The Linden Tree & the Legionnaire

Witch Hammer

Diana Mathur

For Cornelia

The Linden Tree & the Legionnaire series is inspired by the
paintings and accounts of

Kārlis Smiltens

Corporal Smiltens has donated
over two hundred drawings and paintings
to the Latvian War Museum in Riga.

Witch Hammer is fiction.

The characters, their actions and dialogue are conjured in the author's imagination, or are used ficticiously, or are from rants she couldn't help but overhear at the cafe.

1940 Latvia, perilously positioned between two
maniacal, totalitarian dictatorships.

Witch
Hammer

K. Smiltens, 2001.

Prologue

LONDON 1959

*LET IT GO. NOT THAT YOU'RE WRONG, but for
your own sake, lest you go mad. Let it go. There's no
point plotting revenge.*

"I'm not plo—Mama! I just keep track—" He tipped the
metal folding chair on its back legs, balancing against the
small table.

Expecting justice is a waste of time.

His mother was a broken record. Predictably, her next topic
would be…

Isn't there a girl? Someone—

"Yah. I have friends," Kārlis claimed, voice rising with
spirit. "Remember when Stalin died? How we met at the pub
and drank vodka and sang late into the night." Kārlis felt the
corners of his mouth turn up and he crooned with chesty force,
"I threw flowers in the Dauga to send greetings to my girl, ta
da da da …"

The ballad bounced off the walls and the small, dim room seemed to close in and suffocate the singing that waned to agitated foot tapping. "But it costs money to go out," *Kārlis pointed out.* "So I don't often see those knuckleheads from the displaced persons camp. Anyway, they are moving like a stagnant pond." *He quaffed the contents of the shot glass and stared stoically at the wall until the burn of his throat mellowed.* "Well, it's hard to get traction in a new country, Mama. Don't I know it."

They drink too much.

"Because it's hard. We got nothing. Who wants us?" *Kārlis slammed his fist down on the table, making the bottle and ashtray rattle.* "They call me Charlie here. Mama." *He poured another shot, feeling punchy.* "The name Kārlis is too foreign for them." *He relit a cigarette butt that had a few more drags.* "And I don't want to be an outsider. So I'm Charlie."

You drink too much.

"My three best friends are beer, vine and wod – I mean vodka. Yah, yah. Vodka. The English make the v-sound where we would say a w, and vice-verse. Wice-werse. Ha ha ha. We should speak English. Don't sound like a stateless squatter! Remember to switch Vs and Ws." *He was nearly shouting. Why was that? Oh, who cared?*

Find a nice girl and settle down, Kārlis.

"Charlie. I'm Charlie. Mama, and if you're going to be cliché," *Kārlis shifted his chair, breathed heavily and made a point to enunciate,* "then I would rather discuss worldly affairs with Papu."

His parents stared into the room, black-lined figures Kārlis had painted on the wall. Angry slashes of black next to his mother marked the botched attempt to recreate his sister's face.

"As you know, the Communists want to build a wall, Papu." *Kārlis blew a stream of smoke.* "To stop those poor *fools fleeing East Berlin. A wall!" He snorted with scorn. "What is this, the middle ages? Throughout history walls keep invaders out. Never before has a regime built a wall to keep people in, to keep its own people from getting away." Kārlis shook his head, stubbing out the butt. "Border guards in three hundred watch towers will shoot you dead for trying. But I would do it. Wouldn't you, Papu?"*

His father's effigy, sporting a spiffy goatee, a gold chain draped from his vest pocket, and a permanent jolly expression suggested he would make the daring run.

"I can't hear you," Kārlis shouted. "Talk louder. Into my good ear."

Someone pounded on the other side of the wall.

Kārlis nearly fell out of his chair in shock. Heart thumping, he stumbled toward the window, switching off the lamp and flattening himself against the wall, chilled with clammy fear.

Yelling on the other side of the wall, in English, cursed Kārlis.

He snickered, still cringing. It was the ignoramus next door! Not the "knock at night". Ak tu kungs. Kārlis laughed at his own melodrama. Pretty sure the peals were weirdly high-pitched. He could never trust his ears after that damned shrapnel. It's all right, Mama. I'm jittery as hell. That's all. Overly vigilant. Wigilance, vigilance, wigilance. It's normal. Shell shock can take a lifetime. The cure is meat! Eating meat is what broke through the darkness, Mama.

Outside the window, snow blanketed the bleak London outskirt where refugee farm laborers like Kārlis were housed. Mist dulled the black sky, hiding stars. Kārlis stared up anyway, knowing they still shone beyond his view, somewhere in space, where Sputnik circled, souring even the sanctity of the heavens.

"Do the NKVD watch us from space, Papu?"

They're the KGB now.

Kārlis watched the sky with eerie deaf-ear dullness before turning back to his parents.

"I will do what's necessary, Papu," he whispered. The promise sounded like a muffled buzz within his skull. "Don't worry. I'm patient like a spider. One day I'll settle accounts."

He leaned against the wall and whispered, "Killing doesn't count in a war, Mama. Not if you're a soldier. God help me, it doesn't count."

K. Smiltens, 1947.

- 1 -

THE CORNER HOUSE
RIGA, LATVIA
22 DECEMBER, 1940

KKKGH. THE STEEL DOOR CLANKED again.

Peters Kalnins jerked his head up. He'd fallen asleep.

"Eyes!" shouted the guard with the gloved fist. "I want to see your eyes!"

Sweat dripped from his shoulder blades as Peters rolled onto his back and forced open leaden eyelids. The light bulb, stadium bright, pierced his aching head.

Looming above, the black halo of an NKVD visor hat, with the red hammer-and-sickle cap badge protruded from a set of bulging shoulders. The guard was making a visual sweep of the men laying on the cell floor, and the dozen or so lucky enough to be packed onto the cots hinged to the wall.

Peters stared at the ceiling, still as a slit herring lined up in the fish case, hoping not to meet the guard's gaze. Let it be someone else, Peters prayed. Someone else to sit on the wooden chair at the small desk with the ashtray full of, what were they—ripped fingernails, across from the interviewer with the clipboard, the one with the rubber truncheon lurking just out of view.

Prayer turned to panic. If it was him, what to say?

We just need some information. Then you can go home.

One name. Then they'd let him go.

Needed sleep. Think clear. To know. Who. Or not.

Jackboots stepped closer.

"Spit in their face," wheezed the man heaped in the corner. Without lifting his jaw from the floor, he gave the same advice to each prisoner taken to interrogation. "However small the act. Defy them. Russian scum."

Not such a sacrifice for an old fellow to be crippled for life, Peters thought, but he was seventeen and captain of the hockey team.

The boots stopped at Peters's head. "Name."

"Kalnins," Peters said, praying the guard sought another.

A boot nudged Peters's shoulder. "Get up."

Peters rose unsteadily, catching trousers that fell nearly to his knees. At registration they'd taken his watch and belt and, with a large kitchen knife, chopped off buttons, excised his zipper and sliced his coat lining prior to the cavity search. Clutching his pants in one hand, he followed the guard to the door. Neighbor inmates expanded into the vacated floor space.

The steel door banged again. This time Peters was on the other side, staring through bars down a hall of heavily padlocked doors. Noises from different sections of the compound resounded through the hardened tunnel. An engine revved, gates or chains clanked, shouts and moans mingled in hellish cacophony. He thought he heard a gunshot, but tuned it out, feverishly devising what he'd say as the guard shoved him along labyrinthine hallways.

Peters had survived the last interview only because of a miracle.

"Who at your school is printing leaflets?" the agent with the truncheon had asked, studying Peters's reaction.

Could they see his cheeks burning? Hear his guts liquefy? Peters knew the answer. Vilz Zarins was the culprit, Peters's friend since kinderhood. And Kārlis Pērkons, another buddy, illustrated the leaflets with cartoons ridiculing Stalin. The students met secretly at Jekabs Leopolds's family bakery. They had tried to persuade Peters to help them print the secret newsletter *Free Latvia*, along with Eriks Gailis, Hugo Krumins and Sniedze Krasts. Any one of the names could be his ticket out of the Corner House.

Peters shook his head, wishing it didn't hold the knowledge. The agent's eyes bored into him, trying to read his mind. What would an innocent person do? Peters shrugged in the universal gesture of ignorance. Resisting the urge to loosen his collar, he tried to breathe naturally. That's when he smelled smoke.

Instantly an alarm on the wall started hammering, loud and shrill, right next to the truncheon wielder's head. With a swing of his weapon, he took a giant step away from the clanging bell. It was deafening in the tight space. Peters could've shouted rebel names at the top of his lungs and not been heard.

"What in hell!" the agent with the clipboard appeared to shout. "Go find out what it is."

His partner opened the door. He let pass two uniformed men running down the hall before stepping out, closing the door behind him.

The remaining agent sat across the desk, glaring as if the ear-splitting racket were Peters's fault. Big ears protruded from under the officer's cap. He was one of the *troika* who'd arrested Peters in the park.

The Chekist scowled alternately at Peters, the vibrating bell, the clipboard, the door. "*Проклятье*," he cursed and strode out.

Alone, Peters exhaled and pushed his palms against his ears, thankful for the clanging reprieve.

Time crawled.

He watched the door with dread, wondering if everyone had forgotten him. When it finally opened a different guard entered. With bureaucratic indifference, he tied Peters's hands behind his back, giving him just enough slack to hold up his pants as he shuffled beside the guard down to the cell. By the time Peters found floor space among the other prisoners, the bell had stopped ringing.

The miraculous timing of the fire alarm had saved him last night. What would save him now? He vowed to not give the Russian scum a single name. But how bad would the truncheon hurt? How many whacks before a vital organ split?

"Don't confess! Don't tell them anything!" A woman's voice came through the feeding slot of a dungeon door as he passed. "They won't let you out anyway." She echoed behind him. "All you can do now is protect those on the outside."

Peters nodded, his heart tight as a clenched fist. The guard prodded him up the curving wooden staircase. At the top, Peters's knees went weak as he followed the red, carpeted hallway to the interrogation room.

- 2 -

December 22, 1940
The Summerhouse, Latvia

Kārlis Pērkons had been beaten with a leather strap by a Russian *apparatchik* -- a goon near his own age. Then he'd limped home expecting to find solace, only to get hit with a call-up notice drafting him to the Red Army. There was no escaping the Communist occupation, Kārlis thought, head in hands at the kitchen table. Clearly, Stalin's henchmen had known right where to find him, delivering the military telegram directly to the small village, to the rustic manor set off the forest road, and into the trembling hands of his mother. Kārlis felt fully invaded. He removed his glasses and slumped over the red woven tablecloth. Deita, the house cow, plodded over and nuzzled his swollen, bruised face, no doubt hoping for a carrot.

His mother crossed to the window. "Any word on Peters Kalnins?" she asked, lifting a corner of the curtain and searching the darkness. She did that every few minutes.

"You ever heard of a boy coming home after being arrested?" Kārlis replied, hoping she had, and that the ghastly rumors about interrogation at the Corner House were overblown.

His mother's shoulders slumped.

Kārlis felt the corners of his mouth sag. He didn't expect to see his friend Peters again.

The linden tree outside the window creaked in the wind, heavy limbs waving barren, twig-fingered branches.

"She complains," Tante Agata said, interpreting for the tree. Kārlis's elderly aunt cocked her head toward the creaking boughs, her long gray braid slipping over her shoulder. "A linden stands for justice."

Kārlis's mother left her post at the window. She opened the woodstove, lit a long matchstick, and put it to an oil lamp, invoking the biting fragrance of flaxseed oil. There was no electricity at the summerhouse, part of the rustic charm. Moving to the next lamp, she glanced at the window again and hesitated, as if thinking better of drawing attention to the second home of a capitalist. "No sense lighting up the house like a Christmas tree," she said.

The comment fell heavily. Christmas was a few days away, and there was in fact no Christmas tree. Any of the usual hoopla would be grounds for arrest under Article 58 of the Russian Criminal Code.

"Darkest day of the year," Tante Agata said reverently, emerging from her cabinet of curiosities with a small blue jar. "Solstice. Take your shirt off."

"Ow!" Kārlis said, lifting his sweater over his head.

His mother's eyes widened at his gruesome bruises. "How did this happen?" she asked, pointing to a purple welt over his kidney.

"That Russian ratfink the state assigned to Papu's workshop," Kārlis said, twisting to get a look at his backside. "That Igor Volkov, a spy posing as an apprentice." Ribs were red and swollen where Volkov had kept kicking him.

"He's the reason we left Riga. You crossed him?" His mother slumped against the icebox, aghast. "What were you thinking?"

"Somebody had to stand up to the thug," Kārlis said, embellishing his bravery for Mama's sake. He skipped the fact that his purpose for being at his father's Leather Works in the first place had been to steal materials for Molotov cocktails.

Tante Agata looked through the glasses resting on her wizened beak as if she already knew the whole story. "Bruisewort," she said softly. She smoothed salve from the blue jar over the lacerations on his cheeks and neck, her bony fingers cool and soothing.

Kārlis almost whimpered out loud. "That's where he whipped me with a leather strap," he said, feeling pathetic.

When his elderly aunt pressed a point at the base of his skull, tightness melted from his shoulders. It felt pleasing, the way she methodically pushed a path down his spine, flatly chanting, "The servant attacks with saw and axe, the lumber, stack and cord."

"*Aggh!*" Kārlis cried at the word "axe", feeling like she'd stabbed him with a filet knife.

Tante Agata hesitated, uttering something incomprehensible. "Axial trauma," she declared.

Growing up under her care, Kārlis understood that Tante Agata's mumbles were a mnemonic ditty, part of a routine for examining bone and tissue and recalling remedies. It was how she remembered the forest lore.

She poked every bruise along his throbbing skeleton

before exhaling decidedly. "I'll wrap the ribs." Minutes later she'd pulled a strip of linen around his chest and snugged his heart and wind back into place. "There," she said. "Now sit in my chair."

Kārlis dropped into the cushions of the Queen Anne's wingback by the woodstove, carefully raising his feet onto the small tufted stool. As the throbbing subsided, he retreated into a quiet ward of his mind, nursing his wounds and savoring the peaceful, homey comforts. How much longer before he had to leave?

"It says you're to report for a medical examination," his mother said, rereading the call-up notice by the lantern. The shock of the Red Army telegram still made her dab the corner of her eye with a handkerchief.

"Maybe they will see my injuries and say I'm unfit," Kārlis posited.

"You're not that bad," said Tante Agata, pushing a pouch of warmed linseed under his lower back. "Nothing broken."

Kārlis was disappointed to hear that. Besides wanting to evade the draft, he'd already been composing his version of the beating into a gripping tale that would enthrall Lileja Lipkis. Grave injury might inspire her sympathy. Mediocre injury just underscored the fact that he'd had the snot whipped out of him.

"The master's eye makes the horse fat," Tante Agata said, giving him a cup of tea. Whatever that meant, the infusion and the linseed poultice worked like a charm, sending Kārlis into a calm meadow where his worries didn't follow. The moment was idyllic: flames quietly crackling, the promising aroma of dinner, loving women orbiting him - speculating how many would be home for dinner, Deita contentedly munching grain, dim light gentle on his closed eyes. He wished he could slow down time and stay here forever.

The blissful moment faded as the click of high heels coming down the hall grew louder.

"Here she comes," Tante Agata said.

"Some friction is to be expected," Kārlis's mother replied, sighing. "Two families coping with upheaval under one roof."

Kārlis opened his eyes, suddenly recalling that the Krumins family was now sheltering with them, the Russian occupation having left them jobless and homeless.

"We've no choice but to open our door and do our best." Mama sounded like she was giving herself a pep talk.

The heel-clicking rose to a crescendo and Mrs. Krumins blew into the kitchen like a frigid wind. An ice blue dress matching the color of her eyes swished around her tall, willowy figure. Her white hair was pulled back in a severe bun.

"Can't we light some lamps in here?" she demanded. Evaluating the kitchen activity, she beheld Deita with scorn. "Now that's unsanitary," she said with a sniff. "A heifer in the kitchen. Can't you keep it in the barn?"

Kārlis's mother didn't deign to defend the lovingly raised, impeccably groomed, purebred Latvian Brown.

"I've heard tales," Mrs. Krumins said, "of peasants doting on their cows, but I never expected the wife of a prominent businessman to—"

"*Deita* has a pleasing personality," interrupted Tante Agata.

Mrs. Krumins nodded curtly. "Gracious, boy, you've been through a meat grinder," she said, looking Kārlis up and down. "If you're thumped even before boot camp, I shudder to think how you'll fare in the army."

Kārlis nodded ruefully. He knew from spending

time after school at his friend Hugo's house that Mrs. Krumins was high-strung and had to be handled like a vial of nitroglycerine.

"So the Reds are conscripting our boys now," Mrs. Krumins said. She turned to Kārlis's mother. "Mrs. Pērkons, *Anna*, if I may, you cannot bear up under this dreadful turn of events. So I am here to take charge of dinner. Go fetch a bucket of water, Kārlis."

"Don't get up, Kārlis," his mother said. "That won't be necessary, Mrs. Krumins. Tante Agata has already prepared everything."

Mrs. Krumins winced. "I'll be frank," she said, waving a hand at Tante Agata, who stood by her mysterious cabinet behind a scrim of hanging, dried herbs. "In these troubled times, your old auntie should not act so obviously eccentric. Your little girl will go to school and repeat everything she sees in this house, including that twisty folk craft your aunt practices, putting us all in jeopardy."

Kārlis's mother stopped stirring the pot on the stove and turned to face the visitor. "You needn't concern yourself with my daughter," Anna said, cheek color rising. "*My* family is getting along fine."

"I'm concerned about weird crones coming here to compare notes on ancient nonsense," Mrs. Krumins said. "This vagary is what alarms the Communists. And will bring them down on all of us."

"I'll have you know, my aunt is widely respected for her knowledge of herbal medicine," Anna said.

Tante Agata stood listening, resolute as a steel pole, displaying her wrinkled skin like it was the family's proud banner, determined to defeat the enemy with decoction and broth.

Kārlis's mother pivoted back to a simmering pan of cabbage. "Thank you for offering to help, Mrs. Krumins, but dinner is well in hand."

"Look, I'm not a free-loader," Mrs. Krumins said. "We wouldn't be imposing on you at all if the Communists hadn't ousted my husband from the police force." She was looking at Kārlis, as if repeating her tale of woe for his benefit. "Then they evicted us from our apartment to accommodate a high-ranking Soviet officer. It's very humiliating. I am not accustomed to asking for charity."

Kārlis nodded uncomfortably and moved over to the butcher block to slice some black bread.

"Not another word about it, Mrs. Krumins," said his mother. "Of course you must stay here. Especially since Hugo and Kārlis are such close friends."

"Take some tea to calm your nerves," said Tante Agata, going for her infusion.

"Nothing wrong with my nerves! It's the circumstances that are haywire," Mrs. Krumins said, picking up the call-up notice. "I've come down to give you some advice, Anna." She turned her back to Tante Agata. "It's the least I can do in exchange for your hospitality. The storm has now hit your family like it hit ours." She flicked the Red Army's telegram with relish. "This is just the beginning, mark my words. We must prepare for worse. Small measures will make a big difference in the long run. I notice you already hide the sugar. Don't leave the butter out either."

She whisked the butter crock off the table just as Kārlis was about to dip his knife into it. "I will take responsibility for rationing foodstuffs," Mrs. Krumins went on. "It's the least I can do."

Anna abruptly stood. "Give that boy back his butter this instant," she said, pointing at the crock.

Kārlis's jaw dropped at the tightness of her voice. His mother, always composed and gracious, sounded hysterical. "It's okay, Mama, I don't need it."

"And I do not hide the sugar," Anna said with a

stamp of her foot.

"Not from your family perhaps," Mrs. Krumins said. "It's only natural you would hoard luxury items from outsiders."

Deita mooed.

"Hoarding? That's how you think you've been treated here?" Anna said, nostrils flaring. "That's ridiculous." She flung open a cupboard. "Though frankly I am concerned with a bigger picture than the location of the sugar bowl—"

"You think you know better than me how to manage because I'm homeless," Mrs. Krumins said. "Mark my words hard times are ahead. I don't know why you think you'll be spared."

"You don't know what I think, Mrs. Krumins," Anna said, slamming compartments of the enameled stove in her search for the sugar.

Kārlis couldn't understand why the kitchen had suddenly blown up. One moment, all had seemed civil, two matriarchs fending for their families after losing homes to the Communists. Then they'd snapped, making a dogfight between a Messerschmitt and a Spitfire look courteous.

"Here is the sugar! Behind the canning equipment," his mother said, gathering her skirt. She stepped on a chair and hoisted herself up to the top of the broom closet. The sugar bowl was made of milk glass, with two handles and a tight lid. Holding the closet for balance, she descended, presenting it to Kārlis like a trophy. "Put some sugar in your tea, Karli. Go ahead, as much as you want," she insisted, in a syrupy voice that sharply contrasted the acid tone taken with Mrs. Krumins.

"*Paldies*, Mama," Kārlis said, angling for a heaping spoonful. Talk of rationing made him ravenous.

His mother said, "We have more in the cellar, dear."

Mrs. Krumins said, "You won't for long if—"

"If rationing sugar would keep my son out of the army, believe me, I'd count every grain," Anna cut in. "But it won't. So I'm going to make our days together at home as *pleasant* as possible." She spoke pointedly, eyes boring into Mrs. Krumins, who finally looked away. "Tante Agata, use the Rosenthal tonight, the best china. If we have anything good, let's enjoy it while we're *together*." Anna's voice caught on the word. The handkerchief was at her eye again.

"Sloppy," Mrs. Krumins said, plunking the butter crock on the table, "and sentimental. That's a mistake." She exited the kitchen with the staccato of clicking heels.

"Doesn't she know she's insufferable," said Tante Agata.

Anna sniffed. "That woman was a wreck during good times."

"What's this?" Kārlis said, looking in the sugar bowl. He lifted a glittering, chandelier-style earring. "Diamonds?"

The women glanced at his hand and at each other, as if it wasn't the first time precious stones had been found in the tea service. Anna sat down, crumpling her hankie and picking up the telegram in shaking fingers. "That would be your father," she said, composing herself with a deep breath. "Spending cash like tomorrow there'll be nothing left to buy."

Kārlis stared at the diamonds. Even in the dim room and encrusted with sugar, the stones danced with light. He knew his father traded for gold and jewels on the black market. Obviously Papu had to hide his sneakily purchased valuables somewhere. It gave Kārlis an idea. He downed his tea and went to his room.

K. Smiltens, 1973.

- 3 -

WALKING CONFIDENTLY INTO THE DARK bedroom, matches in hand, Kārlis kicked something that felt like a steel hammer nailing his little toe. "Ow! *Pie joda*," he cursed, grabbing his foot and hopping, stumbling over something and landing on his tailbone. Merciless pain shot up his spine and thrummed his ribcage.

"What the *kāpost galva* hell?" Kārlis bellowed. He crawled to the lamp, struck matches at the wick and looked around his room, immediately crestfallen.

Someone had rearranged the furniture! His mattress had been dragged off the boxed-spring frame and flopped in the corner, making the room a double. The floor was stacked with boxes. Punctilious labeling suggested Hugo's neurotic mother had moved in her son to share Kārlis's room.

At that moment, Kārlis realized how he'd cherished an expectation for privacy. He'd looked forward to being inside these four tight walls, where he could grieve for his friend Peters, arrested and possibly tortured, and digest the shock of being attacked and conscripted, and await news of his friends, whether they'd successfully firebombed the Corner House, or if they'd been caught, and all the other dung flung at him lately that needed thinking about.

Ak tu kungs. He sunk against the wall wanting to cry. He wouldn't even finish high school now, and that meant no Art Academy either. The future was in ruins. What a joke to think his bedroom would remain untouched.

Kārlis stared at Hugo's boxed worldly possessions, drained of momentum for what he'd come to do. Finally he worked up the nerve to see if they'd molested his most personal belongings.

Pushing aside the clothes in his armoire, Kārlis felt around the back of the top shelf. When his hands touched the heavy glass jar, he exhaled in relief, lifting down his collection of silver coins. He held it up, giving the jar a little shake, appreciating the weight of his nest egg. He would bury it. Then if he made it back from the army alive, he would at least have a few ducats to his name. Every single move he made now felt significant, potentially his final act in this mortal theatre, and at the same time everything was utterly meaningless. Still, planning for the future was like having some control in the matter. Dinner was almost ready. He didn't have much time.

Donning a sweater, Kārlis wrapped a towel around the jar of silver and slipped out his window. Freezing air sliced at his cuts as he edged around the stone masonry at the corner of the house. He saw the shovel leaning at its usual post near the kitchen door. Grabbing it, he struck out for the woods, the crunch of snow under his boots.

Kārlis hadn't gone far when he saw an unearthly vision by the light of the moon, lurking mere feet away. He stopped dead in his tracks, crippled with chill, watching. Before him, some hunched, shaggy creature with pointed ears and an upright twig-body careened with eerie energy. He tensed warily, ready to defend himself with the shovel, when a thin, cracking voice, uttered,

As I was going to war
I cut a cross in the oak,
So that father and mother shouldn't weep,
So that the crossed oak should weep

"Tante Agata," Kārlis said, exhaling in relief. "Are you—"

Kārlis could barely discern his great-aunt under her furs in the moonlight. She was fruitlessly tugging a rope tied to a log. A few meters behind her wandered Deita.

"Are you trying to drag a yule log?" Kārlis asked.

"Kārlis, I need your help," Tante Agata said. "This is too heavy for me."

Still processing the bizarre sight, Kārlis made no move to help her.

"When combating the powers of darkness, use your strongest weapons," Tante Agata said at his hesitation. "Be a good boy and pull this log around the property. Then bring it inside and burn it. Though it won't be a proper bonfire. We must do what we can to end the scourge of the last year."

Kārlis grimly accepted the rope held out to him. He'd do anything to reverse the Communist annexation of six months ago.

"And you better wear this," she said, pulling something bulky from her apron pocket.

"Do I have to wear a mask?" Kārlis said.

"Next year's fortunes depend on it," replied Tante Agata, holding up a shroud of matted yellow yarn, not unlike a dust mop.

"Can't I wear your wolf mask?" Kārlis said, now that he could see the pointy ears of the fur cap tied under her chin.

"Too small for you. But your Uncle Visvaldis always wore this haystack disguise or went skyclad."

Banishing the vision of his late elderly uncle cavorting naked in the moonlight, Kārlis pulled the yellow yarn wad over his head. He thought Tante Agata, who looked simultaneously frail and wild, should probably get inside the house.

"It's important you are thorough," Tante Agata said. "Now go on. I'll fool the evil spirits," she said, meaning she would handle noisemaking and *daina* incantation. "And mind you," she added as an afterthought, "don't run from Death. If you dance with Death during winter solstice, you'll not die during the next year."

She'd put a finger on his greatest fear.

"Okay, I'll do it," he said, injuries complaining already. Trudging away with the log, he was suddenly overwhelmed by a clutch of concern for the old bird. "Auntie," he said, turning back to her. "Don't let the houseguests see you mumming, all right? You can't trust anyone, you know that?"

"Ha! You mean Mrs. Krumins?" Apples rose on Tante Agata's cheeks. "Don't worry about her. Or the Communists either, for that matter. The deep lore has survived many burning times. Some even worse than this."

The comment troubled Kārlis. Right now armed NKVD agents were posted a kilometer away at the rail platform. If one happened to see Tante Agata in her wolf mask he'd put her down like a mad dog. "But Auntie, Mrs. Krumins is right. The Russian criminal code is brutal. If you attract attention or are different—"

"This is nothing new, Kārlis," Tante Agata said. Her voice no longer sounded crackly, but like part of the wind. "Today it's Article 58. Yesterday it was *Malleus Maleficarum*."

"Mal— what?"

"*The Witch Hammer*. A hunting manual, from a different era but with the same premise, exterminating anyone daring to wear her own shoes. You're a good boy, Kārlis. In fact, you're a man now," Tante Agata said, turning to go in. "Do as you know."

Kārlis felt a tender tug as he watched the old lady forge a path back through the snow, and exhaled deeply, his heart held by her linen bindings. He hadn't planned on a solstice masquerade, but under the circumstances it seemed the right thing to do. His soul was in turmoil. Why question the remedies of the ancients? Besides, this was a perfect excuse to be outside to bury his treasure. If anyone asked where he'd been, he could honestly say he'd gone mumming.

Kārlis tromped into some trees, trailing the log behind. Finding it impossible to dig a hole in the frozen ground, he had to settle for pulling up some floorboards in his mother's garden gazebo. He buried the jar of silver shallowly, but it was well hidden after he replaced the boards.

Then, ribs throbbing, he honored his word to Tante Agata and dragged the yule log from one end of the property to the other, without cutting corners. He pulled the herb-entwined stump at the end of the rope past the well, through a naked birch grove all the way to the river. On the way back he overshot the house, circumvented the dark and forgotten carriage shed, and went nearly to the public road before stopping to rest. Paws scurried overhead, a pine marten perhaps, traipsing the bough's silhouette against the silver sky. Kārlis wanted to absorb every detail of his childscape. You never really saw a place until you knew you wouldn't see it again, he thought. By the time he'd pulled the log back to the kitchen door, he could no longer stand the pain of the rope against his bruised ribs, but it felt good to take back charge of his life.

Picking up the log was painful. Arms full, Kārlis pushed open the back door to the kitchen, sensing with gladness that the house was full of arrivals. His father was home. Still in his suit, Janis Pērkons leaned against the butcher block, the outline of his goatee, usually precise as a razor's edge, was smudged by a long day's stubble-shadow. Kārlis's mother and wide-eyed little sister clustered around Papu. They stopped talking when Kārlis came in, staring at him.

"You look funny," his sister said, gawking, no doubt, at his swollen, bruised eyes.

"Good evening to you, too," Kārlis said, stomping snow off his boots.

It felt awkward facing Papu. Kārlis hadn't seen him since the night before, when his father had stood by watching the Russian bounder, Igor Volkov, mop the floor with Kārlis's beaten carcass. His father had not intervened, afraid of the consequences of defying the Soviet machine. Now with his mother and sister present, Kārlis realized that his reckless actions had endangered the whole family. How would they get along if the NKVD arrested Papu?

"Sorry about that fracas last night," Kārlis told his father.

"Doesn't matter, son. The business is gone," Janis Pērkons said. "Nationalized."

There wasn't time to digest the grave news before his father caught him in a rowdy bear hug, crushing the log against Kārlis's ribs and lifting him off the floor. "I understand the army has inquired after your health," Janis said.

"Ow! Papu! My ribs," Kārlis cried, struggling to get free.

His father released him. "Did you tell them you're Bolshephobic and don't qualify?"

"Yah, yah." Kārlis didn't feel like joking about his doomed future. The heavy log gave him an excuse to move quickly through the kitchen, barely pausing to exchange knowing nods with Tante Agata.

Cutting through the dining room, Kārlis's progress was hindered by the houseguests, the entire Krumins family huddled in meeting. Kārlis nearly bumped into Mrs. Krumins, who, her back to Kārlis, was busy scolding her white-headed spawn. "Just because the Pērkonses go out in the forest at all hours, does not mean you are allowed to."

Hugo, a practiced expression of deference on his pale face, looked past his mother's shaking index finger to greet Kārlis.

Kārlis was relieved to see him. Hopefully that meant the rest of the firebomb detachment had also made it back.

"And wipe off that lipstick, young lady," Mrs. Krumins said, swiping at Elza with a napkin. "You do *not* want to stand out from the crowd."

Elza, her long hair in obedient braids, looked like she had a saucy retort on the tip of her tongue, but she saw Kārlis and clamped her mouth shut, staring like she'd never before seen a man carry wood.

Mr. Krumins had, for some reason Kārlis could not fathom, grown mutton-chop sideburns since his eviction from the police force. He was out of his league in the wife-daughter lipstick dispute and, watching Kārlis struggle under the log, he was oblivious that his portly figure blocked Kārlis's path.

"*Sveiks*," Kārlis told the Kruminses.

The houseguests stared stupidly as Kārlis tried to squeeze past, like *he* was the one intruding on *them*.

No wonder everyone's gaping, Kārlis realized. He was big news, notorious. Been in a fist-fight with a Communist. Drafted. Future scuttled. Just thinking of it all was exhausting. He pushed by, carrying the log toward the fireplace in the front room.

Hugo followed in his wake, using Kārlis as a vehicle to get away from his mother.

"So did you do it?" Kārlis asked over his shoulder.

"Can't talk about it here," Hugo muttered, with the irritating superiority a little knowledge can give a fellow.

A nod of the head wouldn't be *talking* about it, Kārlis thought, disgruntled and feeling outside the club. He was, after all, an integral part of the Corner House scheme, even though he hadn't actually thrown a bottle bomb. Kārlis was a founding member of the Nonchalants, a seven-member secret society formed the previous day to thwart the Communist takeover. "If not for me, there wouldn't be any Molotov cocktails to throw," Kārlis grumbled. It was he, for St. Peter's sake, who'd stolen the combustibles, and got beaten up in the process, which was why he couldn't take part in the actual strike. *Ak tu kungs!* He was as vital to the campaign as Hugo, that smug prig.

"Nice haystack disguise," Hugo said.

Kārlis halted in his tracks. He'd forgotten he was

wearing the stupid hat. Is *that* what people were staring at? He was a spectacle! A beaten, bloodshot idiot in a foolish wad of yellow yarn. He shifted the log to yank the mask off, otherwise ignoring Hugo.

At the mantel, Vilz Zarins slouched commandingly in her black leather bomber jacket, a jubilant glow on her cheeks. Her dark hair was parted sharply down the middle, waves etched by fresh, comb lines. She saw Kārlis coming with the log and stood aside.

"Whatcha wanna know, Karli," Vilz said. Her smile activated dimples that divulged what Kārlis wanted to know.

She'd done it.

Kārlis dropped the log at the back of the grate, inciting an eruption of sparks. He didn't mention that he was fighting the Communist scourge with Tante Agata's yule log, which would sound anemic compared to lobbing actual firebombs. He nodded at Vilz and Hugo, somewhat awed, somewhat jealous of the heroism that must intoxicate them after committing a bona fide act of rebellion.

"Did you do it?" blurted Sniedze Krasts, horning his way into the ring like a pushy elf. "Did—you know— the bottle things, did they work?"

Kārlis cringed. He'd forgotten for a moment that Sniedze, the youngest of the Nonchalants, was even there. Kārlis had been obliged to invite Sniedze home with him so the clumsy kid, who idolized the older boys but had a disastrous habit of saying whatever popped to mind, wouldn't ball up the operation.

"We sent a burning message to our Russian overlords," Vilz said quietly, her pupils large and shiny. She stood taller. "Seriously, the magnitude of the blast caught me off guard, wouldn't you say, Hugo? That's one lesson learned. Those little bottles go *ka wumph*."

"It's a miracle if we got away with it," Hugo whispered, his drawn white face looking furtively into the corners of the room. "You're lucky you weren't there, Kārlis. Lucky you're the pen-and paper type."

Kārlis adjusted his spectacles, irked. *The pen-and-paper type indeed!* Look who's talking! Hugo was slated to be valedictorian of their high school class.

Vilz looked oddly at Hugo, too. "It'll be easier next time," Vilz told him, with chilling confidence.

Kārlis turned his gaze to the burning yule log, hoping to heaven there'd be no next time. This was death penalty-level mischief. The Bolshevik scheme to communize the world did not include taking flak from impetuous adolescents.

"So where's Jekabs? Wasn't he in on it?" Sniedze wanted to know, again talking too loudly. "And Eriks?"

Vilz and Hugo exchanged a look. A froisson of intuition rippled over Kārlis's skin, making the hair stand up.

"Jekabs went home," Vilz equivocated. "Doing business as usual at the family bakery." She looked around the room before saying, "Eriks didn't show."

Kārlis felt the pressing weight of a heavy premonition. For a moment it was hard to breathe. "But the whole crazy plot was Eriks's idea!" he whispered.

"Did he *disappear*?" Sniedze asked.

Ice formed in the pit of Kārlis's gut. *Disappearing* was a national epidemic.

"We don't know what his problem is," Vilz whispered, with markedly less swagger.

"Sheesh," Sniedze said, suddenly breathing noisily. "The Commies are picking us off quick. That's Peters, Kārlis and Eriks." He counted on fingers. "Yesterday we were seven intrepid Nonchalants. Now we're already down to four!" He looked around at faces as if trying to foresee the next vacancy.

"I'm still here," Kārlis said, pushing Sniedze's shoulder. "Can't you count?"

"Maybe Eriks chickened out," Hugo said, dourly. "Or met a girl. Yah, knowing Eriks, that's what happened."

"Yah," Vilz said, lowering her head. "Let's not jump to the worst imaginable conclusion.

K. Smiltens, 1953.

- 4 -

RIGA

ERIKS GAILIS LAY ON THE SMALL BED, muscles twitching in angst. Wherever his mind turned he found something he'd screwed up. He'd talked his friends into throwing Molotov cocktails at the Corner House, and then stood them up. But only because the NKVD had come to his door and he'd had to run for his life. His escape had been a triumph of sorts, except for stupidly leaving the Molotov cocktail behind, in plain view, for the Cheka to find, conveniently giving them evidence that would condemn his parents to death. Inwardly cringing, Eriks clutched handfuls of hair and rocked silently, choking down an animal cry. Sleep was impossible. It would be better for everybody he cared about if he didn't even exist.

He swung his feet to the floor and sat up, reaching to turn on the lamp. Now look. The bandage on his scraped-up hand had come loose and he'd smeared blood all over Mrs. Barons's sheets. Great. She'd been unwilling to hide Eriks in the first place, only reluctantly going along with her husband's heroic impulses. Eriks tightened the gauze bandage and dabbed at the linens, just making it worse.

Eriks exhaled at the futility of it all, looking around at the flowered wallpaper. So this was Zelma Barons's bedroom. He really hadn't known her that well in school, she being one of few to resist his charms. The little mirror propped against her desk was sweetly modest compared to the crystal-laden vanity table where Eriks's mother preened. *Used to preen,* he reminded himself, bitterly. He helped himself to a comb and tugged it roughly through his unruly mane.

There was a quiet knock. The door opened and Zelma's father poked his head through the crack, the freckles on the massive blond ever unexpected. "Good, you're up," Mr. Barons said, in a low voice. "Nearly time to go."

Eriks glanced at the window. It was still dark outside.

"Here, you can wear these," Mr. Barons said, tossing Eriks a pair of gloves and a well-worn fedora.

Eriks dressed and joined the Baronses in their small kitchen where Mr. Barons was gulping the last of his coffee. A cup had been poured for Eriks, but he only pretended to sip it, already too jittery as he followed Mr. Barons from the safety of the apartment, hoping to exit the Cheka-infested building unnoticed. By way of good-bye, Mrs. Barons pushed a paper bag lunch into his hands.

In the stairwell, they fell in behind some other pre-dawn workers. Eriks raised his collar and lowered the fedora. He steeled himself before crossing the brightly lit foyer, where the NKVD stood around, one holding his rifle in a casual one-handed grip, others sprawled in lobby chairs watching the departing residents with jaded eyes. Eriks felt sure his shaking legs gave him away, announcing that he'd defied their fellow goons last night. But somehow he made it past Stalin's secret police and into the biting, dark morning air.

Outside, tall apartment buildings boxed in the avenue, towering above the overhead wires that powered the trolley system. Eriks, eager to get far away fast, was relieved to see the shaky headlight of the streetcar rumbling toward him. He boarded behind Mr. Barons, nudging between strangers, one hand clutching his lunch bag and the other grabbing the hat-level handrail as the trolley lurched. He felt keenly aware of moving in the wrong direction, further away from home. Blocks passed, buildings lost bourgeois art nouveau garnishes, looking utilitarian under sparsely spaced streetlights as Eriks rode an unfamiliar route toward a shadowy vanishing point. This was someone else's life, he thought, finally getting off in an industrial district, a section of Riga he'd never seen.

"Darkness in our favor," Mr. Barons muttered, leading Eriks into a lumberyard.

Eriks had never been so grateful for the winter solstice, for the cloaking gift of the year's darkest day. He followed Barons along an angular walkway smelling of sawdust and machine oil, past mammoth piles of timber, appreciating Mr. Barons's responsibility as foreman here, and thus the magnitude of the risk he was taking for Eriks's sake. They stopped behind the shed nearest the railroad tracks. Farther down the tracks, a light bobbed in the fog. Someone swinging a lantern? Other than that, Eriks saw no one.

"We're going for that one," Barons whispered, pointing to a rail car loaded with milled lumber. "There's a hiding place in that wood stack. A couple of boys are already stowed there. You'll ride about two hours and slip off near a large dairy at the edge of the forest. Caleb'll show you. At an immense stone barn." Mr. Barons turned to look Eriks in the eye. "They'll let you stay there, but you'll have to earn your keep."

Eriks nodded sheepishly. Mr. Barons had already pegged him as a useless lug.

"When you get there," Barons said, his tone softened, "give this to my daughter." He passed an envelope to Eriks.

Eriks folded the unmarked missive and slid it in his pocket.

"If you have resisted arrest as you said. And if your parents have indeed been picked up," Barons said, "well, then this is the best situation I can recommend for you."

Eriks nodded bleakly. *Picked up.*

"The only option really," Mr. Barons said. "Fare well, son."

"*Paldies*, Mr. Barons," Eriks said, sad at breaking the tether.

"Let's go." Barons strode across the exposed lumberyard to the tracks.

Ignoring his clamping guts, Eriks followed Mr. Barons out into the open. It was only about fifty meters to the train, but he'd broken a sweat by the time he reached it. Hoisting himself onto the flat-bedded railcar, just like Mr. Barons had done, he stayed low, while Barons knelt before what appeared to be a solid load of lumber and began shifting pieces.

Eriks kept his eye down the tracks, at the light bobbing in the fog, probably a watchman.

"In here," Barons whispered.

Eriks crawled under some planks, and through an opening. The loaded lumber had apparently been cut in various lengths and stacked to create a hollow in the center. In the pitch black, Eriks couldn't tell the dimensions of the hidey-hole. He maneuvered from crawling to sitting, folding his limbs and ducking his head, cramped and tight-chested, unsure where to put his legs so they wouldn't bump the bodies he sensed nearby in the dark.

The hole closed with a thud, making Eriks's heart pound. He breathed hard and to his relief found there was plenty of cold air coming in through cracks. But the timber could shift and crush him like a bug, he thought, lightheaded with anxiety.

"*Sveiks*, mate," whispered a fellow, calming Eriks immediately. The voice sounded completely unworried, belonging to someone about Eriks's age.

"*Sveiks*," Eriks said.

"I'm Caleb," said the voice. "That's Kristaps."

"How many Cheka out there?" the one called Kristaps demanded, in a higher, probably younger, whisper.

"I didn't see any," Eriks replied. "Just a watchman or someone with a lantern down—"

"Quiet," Kristaps snapped.

Eriks stopped talking. He couldn't hear anything but the shuffle of someone's shifting legs.

"You didn't see them, but they're there," whispered Kristaps. "They're everywhere."

Great, Eriks thought. Just when he'd thought the situation couldn't get worse, he was now boxed in with a bossy paranoid. He settled back, bumping his head against a beam. "Where you fellows from?" Eriks asked. He'd detected an accent in the older boy.

"Poland," said Caleb. "Got out a year ago when Nazis tried moving us to the ghetto. Met Kristaps here in Riga after his parents were deported."

Ghetto? thought Eriks. *Deported?*

"Got anything to eat?" Caleb asked.

Eriks pushed Mrs. Barons's lunch toward the voices. He wasn't hungry. Someone crackled the paper bag with alacrity, and then it went silent.

"Why were your parents deported?" Eriks asked the younger kid.

"Teachers," came the reply, sounding from a full mouth. A second later the kid said, "Now zip it 'til the train gets moving. They're out there."

Eriks shut up, leaving a tortuous silence. Teachers had been deported. His parents had been *picked up*. He felt sick: twisted guts, the chills. He'd heard rumors like these, but they'd always seemed so distant, other people's problems. He wasn't political. Now that he was the victim, he was outraged that no one did anything to help them. Where were the police, or God, or America? He'd been so stupid, actually ridiculing his friend Vilz for trying to organize resistance with a secret newsletter. While Vilz had been taking a stand, Eriks had been drinking shot glasses of Black Balsams and playing jazz with girls who shared his be-merry-for-tomorrow-we-die mentality. He was disgusted with himself.

He'd change.

Finally, the train began creaking down the tracks, jostling the stowaways against their hardwood hideout.

Caleb shifted his sitting position and quietly asked, "You got a gun, mate?"

"A what?" Eriks was shocked by the question, then embarrassed to be shocked.

"A gun. Do you pos-sess a fire-arm?" Caleb enunciated each syllable like he was speaking to a simpleton.

"No," Eriks said.

"Oh, well." Caleb sighed. "Me neither."

"Me neither," Kristaps echoed.

I should hope not, Eriks thought, grateful he was not journeying with an armed and unstable gradeschooler.

"Guess you'll be running errands with us then," Caleb said.

There was a movement. Eriks sensed Kristaps had kicked Caleb into silence.

"What're you talking about?" Eriks said.

"Hey, we're probably in the forest now," Caleb said, instead of answering. "Let's go up top and twist a weed."

A wiry figure snaked past Eriks in the dark, opening the woodpile to a rush of cold air.

"What errands?" Eriks persisted as Caleb also crawled toward the opening.

"Oh, you know," Caleb said, noncommitally, "delivering groceries and what not."

The sky seemed bright as Eriks's head emerged from the faux lumber-stack hideout. He grabbed at boards for balance, taking a moment to get his sea legs before climbing onto the wood, as the other boys had done. Ears blasted by a daunting *whoosh* of cold pine air, he thought he caught the tail of their conversation, Caleb saying, "—but Barons wouldn't have sent him if he wasn't all right."

Eriks climbed over to where Caleb and Kristaps sat, sheltering a match between their hunched shoulders. By its flame, he finally got a look at his traveling companions.

The swarthy, taller one was no doubt Caleb. He had a good start on a moustache and wore circular wire glasses. Uncut hair supported his claim of being on the run for a year. Under a battered fleece jacket, his flannel shirt was unbuttoned low, despite the freezing torrent of air. He returned Eriks's stare with a stream of smoke, offering him a lit, hand-rolled cigarette.

Eriks took a drag, sensing the other boys sizing him up. By his shiny shoes or his alpaca-blend, herringbone weave, double-breasted, imported overcoat, they might conclude he was some cotillion ninny. It was time to establish his credentials. Pointing to his shoulder, Eriks said, "Look here. That's where a bullet grazed me."

Caleb leaned over to look, but it was impossible to see the broken coat threads in the dark.

Eriks went on, "The Riga NKVD was shooting at me." It seemed these bumpkins ought to be impressed by the big-city secret police. "I barely escaped by climbing down the drainpipes of a five-story building. That's how close I came to dying last night." He passed the cig back to Caleb.

"Whew!" Kristaps whistled. "You truly caught some Cheka heat there." The kid's voice had a madcap, scoffing ring. "Bet your tailor was furious!"

Caleb laughed.

Eriks felt his color rise. He leaned over to give Kristaps, who was sitting on the other side of Caleb, a warning eye.

Kristaps looked to be ten or eleven. Brown hair poked from his pointy-knit cap. He was muffled up to the cigarette stuck between rosy, wind-whipped cheeks. "Here's where a Soviet mortar blasted my trousers," Kristaps said with a snort. "See the holes?" He poked cricket-knees up through torn pants.

Eriks was about to grab the flyweight by the collar and hold him over the tracks one-handed, when he noticed Kristaps's feet, perched on the wood, sandwiched between sheets of cardboard and wrapped with cloth. Abruptly ashamed, Eriks turned away. It took grit to joke around when you didn't have shoes. The scrapper punched way above his weight.

"Yah, but my tailor's a mean son-of-a-gun," Eriks said, leaning forward to give Kristaps a nod. "He's the real reason I'm leaving town."

Caleb chuckled.

Eriks silently watched the white trunks of a birch forest whip past while the eastern horizon turned gray. Freezing air blasted commonplace ideas from his head. Wheels underneath him oscillated over the tracks, shaking off any hope he had of returning to his warm, vacuous lifestyle.

"So, you trying to get back home?" Eriks said finally, shouting at Caleb to be heard. "Find your family?"

"Hell, no," Caleb said. "You know what Hitler does to Jews?"

Eriks did not want to admit that he did not know.

"I'm lucky to be here in the Baltics," Caleb said, redefining Eriks's understanding of luck. "To Stalin I'm just as undesirable as the next guy, no more no less. The Commies will take my property." He opened his coat to show he had nothing anyway. "Nazis want my head!"

Eriks was appalled. One of his best friends in Riga was a Jew. Did the Leopoldses know about this ghetto business? And Nazis wanting their heads? If Eriks knew one thing now, it was that he knew nothing. But he'd better be a fast learner.

"So where do we deliver the groceries," Eriks said.

Caleb glanced at Kristaps. Then he pointed into the woods, the tip of his index finger poking from a wool glove. "In there," Caleb said. "To some really angry men."

At the moment the train was traversing a stand of Scots pine. Dark, pointy-topped evergreens, stalwart and protective, interlaced the bony white birches.

"I know there's men hiding in the forests," Eriks said, lest his companions think he was a complete rube. "They must be freezing their stumps off. But if it comes down to getting arrested or hiding in the—" Eriks was struck by a sudden thought. "Say, maybe that's why Mr. Barons sent me here, to join up with those kind of fellows."

"Well, unless you got a gun, delivering chickens is as close as you'll ever get to Silent Forest," Kristaps said, and spat.

"Silent Forest," Eriks repeated, trying not to sound like it was the first time he'd heard the name. "How do you find them?"

"You don't," Kristaps said. "That's the point."

"But there must be a headquarters," Eriks said.

"Every renegade band I've met in the forest is acting on its own, as far as I know," Caleb said, returning some salvaged shreds of tobacco to a little tin box. "But all with the same purpose."

"To string up Ivans by the nuts," Kristaps said. Clutching the opening of his thin coat with one hand, he announced, "I'm going in."

A moment later Caleb also scooted back inside the hidey-hole.

Eriks stayed up top, as if the rushing air might blow off the dread that kept settling on him. He didn't know what to do. Growing up in a swanky, family-owned department store had not prepared him for life as a fugitive. But he had to do something, fast. Now that his head was out of the sand, he was going to pay attention.

Riding the rumbling woodpile, Eriks tried to digest everything he saw: where the tracks ran parallel and where they branched off, a water tower in the distance, a power transformer, a bridge, impassable bog, the morning moon over exposed farmland, dense forest, an isolated house. He saw a police station, guards at a roadblock, and a fire on a hill. He noted the names of villages. He desperately watched the passing landscape as if it held the key to his survival, tears freezing at the corners of his eyes.

He would need a gun.

The train slowed to a bare chug, cornering a tight bend. Caleb and Kristaps crawled back out and the three boys watched in awe, the entire length of the train forming an arc. A weak sunrise imbued the fog with a silver glow, dramatically backdropping the churning black smoke of the locomotives. It'd been about two hours since they'd left, or so it seemed to Eriks. He said, "Is our stop coming up?"

"Yah," Caleb said, stretching and looking diverted. He removed his glasses and tucked them in his coat. "But who said anything about a stop?" Caleb was studying the tracks and rocking his weight back and forth. "Pay attention," he said, waving a finger to Eriks. "I'm only gonna show you this once." Then he hurled himself off the railcar in a forward somersault, rolling down the snowy embankment and out of sight.

K. Smiltens, 1947.

- 5 -

"GENTLEMEN." KĀRLIS'S MOTHER WAS COMING at him and his friends with a tray of crystal and a certain look-what-I-have enthusiasm. She had a fresh coat of lipstick in a berry shade, a white chiffon apron, and her brown hair was mounded around her head in elegant swirls, like when she entertained his father's company.

Tante Agata hobbled a few paces behind, carrying a corked flagon made of brown crockery. *Rigas Black Balsams*, the cordial's ornate black-and-gold label had always appealed to Kārlis.

"Mmm, Black Balsams," Sniedze said. "What's the occasion, Mrs. Pērkons? Can't be Christmas since that's not allowed."

His mother's eyes flashed at Sniedze, and Kārlis expected her to scold him, saying that Christmas-talk could get them arrested and, almost as bad, upset Kārlis's little sister. But she smiled at Sniedze with barely a trace of annoyance and set the tray on the sideboard.

"No occasion, Sniedze," Mrs. Pērkons said. "I just think if a boy's old enough to be a soldier, he ought to be able to have a nip of spirits."

"I won't argue with that," Kārlis said, raising eyebrows at Vilz, who was shrugging off her bomber jacket, getting ready to nip.

Tante Agata set the flagon carefully on the tray and turned to face the fire, her gray braid over one shoulder, and long necklaces of chunky amber glowing in the firelight. Her birdlike eyes seemed as hot as the flames while she watched the yule log destruct.

"May I help you with that, Mrs. Pērkons?" Hugo said, stepping over to the tray. "I know how to mix it."

Kārlis's mother said, "*Paldies*, Hugo."

Hugo uncorked the Black Balsams and, with Fred Astaire-aplomb, lifted it high so the viscous black liqueur poured out in a long, thin stream precisely into the slim opening of a crystal carafe. He was stirring in the vodka when the fathers, having ferreted the scent, ambled over.

Mr. Krumins went to the radio, a VEF in a large cabinet standing in the corner, and fiddled at the dials. A tinny voice from far away entered the room.

Kārlis moved closer, trying to block out Hugo's chatter and understand the broadcast, which was in Russian. He couldn't catch the gist, but thought he would at least recognize any mention of the Corner House. Had the Corner House gone up in flames? Had his friends succeeded in burning NKVD headquarters to the ground, resulting in the escape of detainees like Peters? Had they at least inconvenienced the brutes?

Vilz was listening hard, ear toward the tuner. "I swear," she whispered, coming over to Kārlis, "flames were seven meters high."

Kārlis nodded. Vilz wanted to be a journalist.

Accuracy meant something to her.

"I assume you've registered the radio," Mr. Krumins bellowed, "so it's legal."

"Of course," Kārlis's father said, though Kārlis doubted that was true. "Those broadcasts are baloney, anyway. Put on some Strauss."

Hugo had poured his elixir into tiny glasses. Mrs. Pērkons passed them around.

Kārlis waited by Tante Agata until everyone was served.

"Be advised," Tante Agata told him, nodding at the glass. "The Balsams is an erudite distillation. Sometimes called Black Devil, for good reason."

"Thanks for the warning, but I already feel like something on the bottom of a shoe, Auntie," Kārlis said. "Don't think I can feel any worse." It even hurt to lift his toasting arm.

But when everyone else did, forming more-or-less a circle of raised glasses, Kārlis held his up toward his mother, then to the other boys and Vilz, who were all watching one another. It was a silent, grim toast, more of a salute to those *not* there, to a cancelled Art Academy, to a confiscated Leather Works, than a cheer to the remaining Nonchalants, unlike yesterday's reckless vows of rebellious solidarity.

When glasses were already tipped, and before anyone could stop her from being so brazen, Vilz quietly said, "Free Latvia."

Kārlis quaffed the potion in one slug. A fireball burned to the pit of his stomach and flared back up his throat in a toxic cloud. *"Ak tu kungs!"* he said, eyes watering. That hurt. But he sucked it up, refusing to be like Sniedze, who was huffing between a scream and a choke.

A noisy crackle filled the air as Mr. Krumins dropped

the phonograph needle on a record. Trumpets heralded a symphony.

Kārlis realized that he'd been holding his shoulders crunched up tight. He released them with a loud exhale. Then he noticed the shadows, lurching up the walls and onto the high ceiling, lending a gothic quality to the ambiance. Naturally! Being the *summer*house, he'd mainly been here during summer's hours of endless light. But tonight, the winter solstice with its plethora of candles, made the refuge look like the kind of place favored by bats.

His head felt lighter, swaying in three-quarter time with a string section. "What is this?" he asked his father, who was ensconced in the couch, tapping his foot and looking thoughtful.

"Treasure Waltz," said Janis Pērkons.

How could Papu be so calm? Kārlis marveled. The man's life's work was just confiscated. Kārlis had always assumed that *he* would inherit his father's business, not some Russian interloper. That Kārlis never wanted to be a businessman was beside the point. The Leather Works was gone, lost to the likes of Igor Volkov, and here they were listening to Strauss. Strange.

Hugo sallied over with the carafe. "I always say, when life hands you an empty glass, find the person that life has handed the vodka to." He refreshed Kārlis's drink without being asked. "You look like you've been trampled by bulls."

"Never fight ugly people, Karli," Vilz said. "They got nothing to lose."

"I would never fight for my beliefs," Sniedze said, "because I might be wrong."

"Let's eat while it's hot," his mother said, and Kārlis joined the household, following her to the dining room like a polite pack of hungry wolves.

Biruta was already there, climbing over chairs to light candles.

Kārlis sat down near his friends at his mother's end of the table, from where she could hop to the kitchen or gaze at his father over ten place settings of white linen. She set a steaming tureen of pig's head stew before him, and Kārlis was counting his blessings when he heard the click of high heels on wooden stairs.

Mrs. Krumins entered the room, casting a willow tree shadow on the wall. She took in the gathering with inscrutable eyes, and said, "Where is Elza?"

Kārlis had not noticed Hugo's sister was absent.

"Stomped out with her lipstick," said Mr. Krumins. "She can't have gone far."

"Surely we're not starting without her," Mrs. Krumins said, directing the comment to Kārlis's mother. "Anything might happen. Hugo, go down to the river and find her."

Hugo started to rise.

"Sit down, Hugo," Mr. Krumins said, pushing a palm out. "We're starting without her." To his wife's eviscerating gaze, he said, "We should not hold up everyone's dinner just because Elza is not on time."

Kārlis's father pulled out the chair on his right for Mrs. Krumins.

She looked at it with doubt before woodenly sitting down. "That's another disadvantage of staying here," she muttered, as Kārlis's father pushed her in. "Practically next door to that Lileja Lipkis."

At the mention of Lileja, a shot of tingle zinged Kārlis's brain.

"She's a fast one," Mrs. Krumins said. "And it's no wonder, raised in a tavern by her father. A bad influence on my Elza." She turned a steely gaze toward Kārlis's mother.

"Bon appétit," his mother said. "Please begin."

"Lileja's not like that, Mama," Hugo said, dishing potatoes. "She's a nice girl. I wouldn't worry."

Kārlis froze, the serving fork midway from the pork platter to his plate. Hugo had just defended his girl. He felt a blast furnace ignite behind his eyes, but he kept cool. Mimicking the others, he dished and passed the purple cabbage, then the sour cucumbers.

"It's not like we're in the city," Hugo said. "Elza and Lileja probably met friends and the time got away."

"That's exactly what I *am* worried about," Mrs. Krumins said. "Hanky panky with her so-called friends in the forest."

"It's normal the youngsters want to get together," chimed Kārlis's father. "Blow off some steam."

"You can't keep her home forever," Hugo said.

"Nothing normal about any of this," Mrs. Krumins said, looking like she'd drank vinegar. "I'll keep her locked in a closet if I have to."

"Please pass the herring," Vilz said.

"And the bread," said Sniedze.

The room went silent, but for the occasional scrape of a chair on the floor, and the clink of silver against china muffled by linen. Kārlis swirled a forkful of pork and potato through the cream on his plate, leaving a pink trail of juice that he sopped up with bread, which he chased down with milk.

Optimism grew with every bite. That was the power of Mama's cooking. He'd miss her the most. He'd miss dinners like this. Looking around the table, he sensed the mood of the company improving, and felt a soft spot for everyone there, for everyone, that is, except Hugo.

Chatter bubbled in small pockets along the table.

Papu was telling a story about a farmer who'd traded him garden produce for leather goods. "So he shows up with a wagon full of plums! Nothing but plums," Janis boomed, refilling the wine glasses of all within reach. "We had plums coming out our ears. How many liters did you put up, Agata?"

"Every jar, glass, and flowerpot in the house!"

His father laughed like Tante Agata had said the funniest thing he'd ever heard. The faces at Papu's end of the table were relaxing, Kārlis noted with admiration. Papu had changed their orbits by sheer force of personality.

You don't appreciate a thing until you know you won't be having it again, Kārlis thought looking around the table, like chit-chat and jokes at dinner. Simple stuff, but really as nourishing as any food they ate. He wished he'd inherited his father's gift of gab. Conversation was like throwing a lifeline to someone. Folks talking over a matter at dinner were weaving a net of sanity, however temporary, saving everyone seated there.

"Anna, you're a marvel," his father said, waving his fork and smiling wolfishly.

His mother nodded.

"Indeed," Mr. Krumins added, "Especially with shortages being what they are."

His little sister was under the table, crawling through a forest of legs in pursuit of the cat.

"Pour me some milk," Kārlis said, pushing his glass toward Vilz.

"I've heard in the army they expect you to pour your own milk," Vilz said, complying.

"That could be a problem," Kārlis said. "Once poured, who will raise it to my lips?"

"Seriously, Kārlis. It's outrageous," Vilz said. "Your call-up notice absolutely violates international law. An occupying nation may *not* forcibly conscript citizens of said occupied country."

"Uh-huh," Kārlis said, head starting to hurt.

"I was about your age when I was drafted into the Czar's Imperial Army," Hugo's father said, over a mouthful of food. "Boys become men. Men become soldiers. Show some backbone."

"Weird that Kārlis is one of *them* now," Hugo said, philosophically. "Guess we better watch what we say, right?" Hugo chuckled like he was such a comedian.

Under the table, Kārlis squeezed a piece of bread in his fist. Hugo had given voice to a vague, lonely idea gnawing Kārlis's stomach lining. More than the physical deployment, the Army could pit him against his home folk, and them against him. He opened his hand to find a knuckle-shaped lump of dough.

Ting, Ting. Mrs. Krumins tapped her fork against a goblet. *Ting, ting, ting.* Every tap felt like a stab to Kārlis's eyeballs. She stood holding up her glass. Kārlis had spent enough time with the Krumins family to know someone was in for it.

"This may be the last meal we share together before Kārlis goes off to join the Red Army," Mrs. Krumins said. She saw that everyone was suitably sober before gazing into her upheld goblet like it was a crystal ball. "It's just a matter of time until my Hugo will be drafted too." Her speech was speeding up. "Probably tomorrow's mail—or the next day's. My only son. Adding his name to the tragic list with Peters Kalnins and Kārlis Pērkons…"

"Oh, for godssake," her husband said, dropping his fist on the table. "Get a grip, woman."

Mrs. Krumins put the goblet down. "How can you think of eating at a time like this?" She screeched her chair back. "Why don't we *do* something?" Mrs. Krumins threw her napkin on the table and turned her head like she couldn't stand the sight of them.

No one answered her question. Kārlis kept chewing as everyone's gaze followed her clicking heels out of the room and upstairs. Why was only the Crazy Woman talking sense?

"Kārlis, why don't you just run?" Sniedze said. "There's guys hiding in the forests and—"

"That is foolish talk," Mr. Krumins interrupted, planting his hands on either side of his plate. "The Red Army's known to execute whole families, sometimes a whole village related to a deserter." He stood, squared his shoulders and spoke in stentorian tones. "Our only hope lies with Germany." Leaning over the table like a preacher into the pulpit, he directed his advice first to Kārlis then to the rest of the table. "Pray for the forces of Adolf Hitler. Pray to God Hitler crosses our borders soon."

Kārlis interpreted the silence to mean that nobody else felt safe, or foolhardy, enough to tout a political opinion.

"Cross our borders?" Vilz said quietly. "You mean storm through Latvia like he has everywhere else? I'm praying for a sovereign Latvia. Not one overrun with Nazis."

The table was sitting up now, leaning forward. Kārlis wasn't surprised by Vilz's views, which he well knew, but he'd never heard Vilz contradict an elder. He glanced around half-expecting the etiquette patrol to pounce or for Mr. Krumins to grab Vilz by the throat.

Vilz sat, hands in her lap, blue eyes alert, black hair slicked back neatly. She didn't have one line on her face compared to haggard old Mr. Krumins, but she had a kind of authority, probably gained from attending secret meetings and throwing Molotov cocktails.

"In fact, I'd rather we stop praying and start fighting," Vilz said. "The Prime Minister should have issued a call to arms immediately when Russia strong-armed the election. He was wrong telling us not to resist. But it's not too late."

Mr. Krumins crossed his arms, eyes narrowed. "You're a little young to be questioning the prime minister."

"Old enough to remember what it was like to have choice," Vilz countered.

"Lady and gentleman, we're not having this discussion here," Kārlis's father said, standing. "The consequences of loose talk are brutal. I won't permit it in this house."

"The devil himself does not know where women sharpen their knives," shot in Tante Agata, who was circling the table and clearing plates.

Foreheads creased as the diners puzzled over her proverb. Tempers seemed to cool.

"So if it were up to you, you'd send our boys to certain defeat?" Krumins demanded of Vilz, getting in the last word.

Certain defeat. The phrase hardened in Kārlis's stomach like a cold stone.

Vilz said, "No one would die in vain who established for the record, for all time, that Latvia did not go willingly to the Soviet Union."

Die in vain. No, Kārlis would rather die for a good cause. But he didn't want to die at all. Dying is what old people did. He was seventeen and, instead of adulthood, death taunted him from every corner.

"We need some tangible marker, and that's the last I'll say, sir," Vilz said quietly, appealing to Kārlis's father. "Bones on a battlefield. Some major act of rebellion. Something future generations can point to that says this was not the will of a sovereign nation. And it better be something that will stand up against a deluge of brainwashing."

"Where are you getting these ideas?" Krumins said, red in the face. "You sound like some penny-ante statesman, not a high schooler. I already warned you against those meet—" He closed his mouth at the approach of high heels, clicking like the clock on a time bomb.

Mrs. Krumins was back in the room. Kārlis saw his father and the other men rise and grudgingly stood up as well.

"Krumins," said Mrs. Krumins. "Elza is without a chaperone. It's past curfew."

"I'll get her, Mother," Hugo said, looking eager to leave. "Coming Vilz?"

"I'll come too," Sniedze said. "We might see Lileja." His eyes lit up. "And she'll want to know the news from Riga."

Mention of Lileja Lipkis roused Kārlis's heartbeat. He wanted to get up and leave with his friends, but he caught sight of his mother's bright eyes watching him. He had to consider her feelings at the moment. She'd made his favorite meal, after all. His buddies didn't miss a beat though, he noticed, as they loaded into their coats and went out. He might as well be gone already.

Mr. Krumins, grumbling and placating, followed his wife upstairs, leaving just the Pērkonses at the table.

His mother went to the kitchen and came back minutes later, with a warm plate. "Apple cake with vanilla sauce," she murmured, setting the dish before Kārlis. "I saved this especially for you."

"*Ak tu kungs*," Kārlis said, acting enthusiastic. "My favorite!" He had no appetite, but moved the cake around, shoving some down his throat.

He wanted to satisfy his mother's desire to talk, but every topic on Kārlis's mind was either bad news or taboo, and his little sister was listening.

His hours were numbered. He wanted to see Lileja.

"*Paldies*, for the cake, Mama," Kārlis finally said, rising, feeling like a heel. These might be the last moments at home with his family, but he was too distracted to stay. "That was delicious."

Kārlis collected some dishes and took them to the kitchen. He found Tante Agata in the chair by the wood stove, pipe-hand in her lap, mouth open and snoring lightly.

"Leave it, Kārlis," his mother said, following him. "I'll wash up."

As Kārlis buttoned his coat his father came up to him. Janis's beard looked grayer than it had an hour before, if that were possible. "Kārlis," he said in a low voice, "I must warn you again not to discuss anything political with anyone." He seemed to be debating telling Kārlis something else. "Even Mr. Krumins, son. Though he's an old family friend, he has the instincts and training of a police officer and... who knows. It might one day turn out that he has more in common with the local militia than with us. I'm not saying that is the case, and certainly don't repeat it. I'm just saying—" His father sounded tongue-tied, talking with his hands as words eluded him. "Just don't talk to anyone."

"Don't worry, Papu. I trust no one."

As he left, Kārlis heard his father say, "It'll be all right, Anna. The boy knows to get out of the rain."

- 6 -

KĀRLIS COULD SEE BY TRACKS IN THE SNOW that his friends had taken the forest path, no doubt headed to the noble oak. Before crossing into the wall of trees, he looked back at the house. It was sparingly lit, but the stained glass around the front door cast some color on the surrounding carpet of white crystals. The flip of a curtain at the window gave away the presence of his mother, the vigilant lookout.

The forest was desolate, the trail muddy in some places, icy in others. No matter how well you knew a forest, it could be spooky in the dark. When Kārlis arrived at the river's edge, fog was rolling over the water like a convoy of ghost tanks. Ten minutes further, the path skirted a village road where the local Communist militia had erected barbed wire and the sign *Halt or You Will Be Shot!* Maybe the barbarians succeeded in scaring most folks away from the woods,

Kārlis thought, but this forest was part of him on a cellular level, its contours indelibly etched in his mind and muscle memory. He rushed down an outcropping of boulders like they were stairs. Nobody knew these woodlands better than he did after sixteen summers of hide-and-seek. Except maybe Hugo. They'd been as close as branches of the same tree.

How could he have stood the loathsome carbuncle for so long? A bitter taste invaded his mouth and he spat it out. Packing a snowball, Kārlis heaved it at a tree-trunk, wishing the broad bark were Hugo's white face. That felt good. He scooped up more snow and began to pack another one. It felt good to have a face to hate.

He couldn't blame Hugo for everything that had gone wrong. Not for Peters's capture or the derailed Art Academy, not for that despicable Russian who had ambushed him with a whip and stolen Papu's workshop, or for being drafted. But Hugo better think twice before messing with Lileja. Kārlis was going to articulate an understanding with her tonight. Scooping up more snow, he packed the ball harder. Hugo didn't know the first thing about that girl.

Kārlis, on the other hand, had observed his Lileja intently. His muse, she was the constant subject of his drawings and paintings. He could catch her wood-nymph posture and hungry coquettish expression with the flick of a pencil. If you didn't get the essence of someone's face in the first strokes, you might as well give up. No amount of erasing or redrawing could improve it. It was an organic thing, to capture the face. In the process of mastering Lileja's expressions, he'd learned a surprising contradiction about the barkeep's daughter. She could knock a man down with the bat of her eyelashes, but also she was as delicate as a porcelain dish about to fall off the shelf.

The result of Kārlis's studies was his masterpiece, a portrait of Lileja at the beach last summer. He'd given her the portrait during their last visit and in his view that cemented the indefinable something between them. All had been going according to plan until Hugo waltzed in, throwing a wrench in the courtship machinery.

Kārlis heard the voices before he saw them, comfortable low murmurs coming from the noble oak. The tree had a girth of seventeen folk dancers holding hands, and a glorious, spreading crown. The lowest branch supported a wooden swing, a community monument to rites of spring, and a hot spot for youth even when the ropes were frosted with crystals.

"Oh Hugo, your hands are fuh-reezing!" It was Lileja. Hot poison shot through Kārlis's veins. The varmint's hands were on her! He squeezed the snowball to the hardness of a diamond.

Lileja and Hugo were laughing.

"Here, finish it," Hugo said. "Warm us both up."

Eyes accustomed to the dark, Kārlis easily observed the clearing. Moonlight illuminated Lileja sitting on a wooden swing hanging from an oak bough. In front of her, glowed Hugo's silver-white head. The swing had been pushed high and was held there braced against Hugo's waist. Hugo was nestled into Lileja's furs; her long legs, covered in soft wooly stockings and dainty leather snow boots dangled above the ground. The air was foggy around their heads. A low, encroaching cloud veiled the edges of the clearing with intimacy. Lileja tipped her chin up, drinking from the flask.

"This is so dangerous," she said, giggling. "You really have a Moddletoff cocktail?"

"Mm-hmm," Hugo crooned.

Plying her with alcohol! Divulging Nonchalant

secrets! Kārlis was disgusted.

"Thissis what we're drinking?" Lileja said.

"No, no," Hugo said. "We're drinking a mixture of very good quality vodka and Black Balsams."

From his mother's kitchen! The snake thief. Kārlis was livid.

"You see," Hugo explained. "Molotov was dropping bombs on the Finns and calling them bread baskets. So the Finns, like they're playing along with it, invented the cocktail. To go with the Molotov bread basket."

The back-story was lost on Lileja. "Issit in your pockets?" she asked in a gooey voice. "Hmmm?" She leaned into Hugo, sliding her hands around in his coat and pockets.

"Careful," Hugo chided, holding up a milk bottle with a gold fringe fuse. "And no smoking! This could take our heads off." Hugo moved around the trunk of the tree for a moment, like he was stashing the incendiary weapon. Then he came back and held Lileja, or perhaps steadied her, so she wouldn't fall off the swing.

Kārlis approached them rigidly, an angry outsider, aware his disapproval was not stylish. He stood on the opposite side of the raised swing, so Lileja hung between him and Hugo.

"*Sveiks*, Lileja."

Lileja flinched. "Karli. You scared me, shneaking up."

Crossing her legs, she shifted her weight on the swing, taking a more neutral position between him and Hugo. She smelled boozy. "I heard you been through the wringer," she said, touching his arm with a mittened hand.

Hugo said nothing. He made no move to release Lileja and the swing.

An owl hooted from the direction of the river and

was answered by one nearer the village.

"I thought your mother sent you to find Elza," Kārlis told Hugo.

"Vilz and Sniedze are getting her," Hugo said. "Appreciate your concern." Smiling and adjusting his grip on the swing, Hugo said, "I couldn't leave this rare woodland creature alone."

O spare me the poetry, Kārlis thought, longing to wipe the smile off Hugo's face.

"Hugo told me about the army, Karli," said Lileja.

Damn him. Hugo was a bone in his throat. Kārlis did not deserve this aggravation right now.

"What a rotten break," Lileja said. She flung her arm around Kārlis's shoulders, making her sweater askew and showing brassiere straps and milky white skin and collarbones. "When do you have to go?"

Kārlis didn't reply. It was slimy of Hugo to get Lileja drunk like this. Some of the mothers already accused Lileja of being a strumpet or what-have-you, making Kārlis extra protective of her reputation. He'd better get her home before further damage was done.

"And he told me," Lileja said, tittering, "about the haystack disguise." She tried to stifle a laugh and failed, "I wish I could have seen it." Then she burst out, belly splitting, "I adore you, Karli. Ha ha. Oh, ha ha ha! You're such a goofball." She almost fell off the swing again.

Hugo caught her in his arms.

That did it. Kārlis glared at Hugo, his eyes two howitzers. "I heard you say you have a Molotov cocktail," he said, hefting the snowball in his palm.

Hugo couldn't deny it. He'd been caught bragging about it to Lileja.

Kārlis watched Hugo's face carefully. The patrician

features everyone thought were so handsome didn't charm him. Hugo actually had quite thin lips, and a nose like a 30-60-90 triangle from geometry. Hugo glared at him, stubbornly holding his grip on the swing, on Lileja. The clearing was negatively charged like the air before lightning strikes.

"So that must mean you didn't have the guts to throw it," Kārlis said. "Is that the way it happened? At the Corner House? You let the other guys do the heavy lifting?"

A flicker of guilt shadowed Hugo so Kārlis went in for the kill. "Let me guess, you were the first to run?"

"Shouldn't be talking about it here," Hugo said, pushing the wooden plank of the swing into Kārlis's ribs.

Ow. Pain wracked his whole skeletal frame. "I agree," Kārlis said, shoving the swing back at Hugo. "I was surprised to hear your blabbing about it just now."

"Hugo trusht me," Lileja said. "He told me all about what happened to Peters." Eyes filled with tears. "They can't just take him away like that."

"Hugo was the first one to run then too," Kārlis said.

Hugo jammed the swing into Kārlis so hard it knocked him back a few steps, saying, "Isn't what happened bad enough without your *kāpost galva*—"

Stultified with pain, Kārlis somehow regained his balance. He took aim at the white face and heaved the snowball at point blank range, hitting Hugo square between the eyes.

Staggered blind at first, Hugo then moved like a wolverine. Ducking around the side of the swing, he released Lileja, slamming into Kārlis.

Lileja screamed, groping at ropes as the swing zagged loose.

Kārlis was laid out with a jarring thud, never knowing such pain. Hugo was on his chest, icicle fingers at his throat.

Lileja's screams flayed the air.

Kārlis pried Hugo's fingers off his neck and scrambled to his knees. Then he delivered the blow he'd imagined for two days, shocked at the crunch of Hugo's nose under his fist and the immediate slickness of blood on his knuckles. Yah! That's how he should've hit that Russian Volkov! That's how he'd handle himself in the army!

Hugo recoiled, arms to head, blood blotching the snow.

In the next instant all the pent-up bitterness for his butchered life went into Kārlis's fists. He beat Hugo as if the white-haired boy were Stalin himself.

What in hell was Lileja screaming about!

Then the world turned upside-down. Kārlis tumbled over Hugo's outstretched leg, glimpsing bare branches overhead before vision was snuffed in white darkness. Hugo was on his back, twisting his arm. Snow packed his ears as Hugo ground his face downward. Ice scraped. He couldn't breathe. Rising for air, pushed down harder, ribs shrieking. He couldn't worm away or throw Hugo off however he bucked.

Smothering. About to die.

Suddenly the weight came off. Lifted by the scruff of the neck, up and over, Kārlis saw branches again. He lay there on his back, gulping air, arms raised protectively, panting.

Vilz stood over him, her black jacket and sea cap stark against the moonlit fog. "Can't you find a *kāpost galva* Commie to choke?" Vilz demanded, giving a handkerchief to Hugo.

"He's such an ass," Hugo said, holding his nose.

"Well, what if you had to go with the Russian army?" Vilz said. "You'd go crazy, too. Give a brother a *kāpost galva* break." Vilz leaned down, inspecting Kārlis for damage, and picking up his glasses from the snow. "Hugo's not the enemy, you know," Vilz said, brushing off Kārlis's fedora and giving it to him.

Vilz looked from Kārlis to Hugo with disdain, "Wouldn't they love to see you two at each other's throats? Two less Latvians for them to beat down." She patted her pockets until she found cigarettes. Raising a foot she stamped the earth, striking the match along the side of her pants.

"What difference does it make," Kārlis said, getting up gingerly, holding his ribs and quashing the desire to cry. If he couldn't even defend himself against Hugo, how would he survive the army?

Sniedze appeared suddenly, his approach to the clearing unnoticed. "We heard screams," Sniedze said. "What's going on?"

Elza was several strides behind him. She was willowy like her mother; with the same silver-white hair as Hugo, but waist length, zigzagged as if her braids had recently been undone and wild from running.

"What happened?" Sniedze asked. "NKVD?"

Nobody answered. The quiet was finally broken by Lileja's moan. She was draped over the seat of the swing, head hanging, hands and feet brushing against the ground.

Perhaps, Kārlis hoped, she'd been too drunk to notice Hugo grinding off his face.

"Nerves," Vilz said. "We're fighting with each other because we don't dare strike at our real enemy." Her dimples deepened when she dragged on her cigarette. "We got to pull together, *cilvēks*, to bring the Ivans down."

Kārlis stood crookedly fingering his throat. Hugo was bent over, washing blood off his face with snow. Lileja was limp fur, hangdog over the swing. The notion that they might bring down the Ivans was farfetched.

"We have to recapture the spirit of the Nonchalants and stand together," Vilz said, trying to turn the debacle into a pep rally. "All we have is each other."

"You guys were fighting over Lileja," Sniedze concluded, sounding disappointed for missing it. "Who won?"

Kārlis, amid alternating waves of humiliation and euphoria, determined to keep to his plan. Going to the swing and supporting her waist, he lifted Lileja's shoulders, parting the curtain of gold hair to find her face. She looked slack and slobbery, and red as a beet from hanging upside-down.

"Let's go," Kārlis said. "I'm taking you home."

Lileja popped up like an unsteady rag doll come to life. Grabbing the rope, she said, "Yah. I have something to give you, Karli. I have to give you before you go 'way."

"Fine," Kārlis said, secretly soaring with delight. "Then let's hit it."

"Kārlis," Hugo said, reluctantly. "I want to forget this if you do—"

A beam of a light invaded the clearing. It streaked over Hugo and oak branches and the paralyzed figures of Elza, Vilz and Sniedze, and then swept away.

"Стой, или вы будете расстреляны!" The words were incomprehensible, but the shout was close, practically in the clearing with them.

Everyone scattered like shot.

Kārlis grabbed Lileja and tried to lead her into hiding. She stumbled and fell to her knees. He bent down and braced her arm across his shoulders, leveraging her to her feet, her weight a knife between his ribs. Gripped in panic, he trudged her behind the vast girth of the noble oak. She wrapped her arms around the huge trunk, as if clinging to the only stationary object in the universe.

"Shpinnin'," she said, face white. She wasn't going to make it further.

Digging his fingers into the crevices of the bark, Kārlis cat-climbed up the trunk to the lowest bough. He hung, bouncing, until the lumpy accumulation of snow on the limb slid off in a gloppy, white sheet. Dropping to the ground, he saw he'd covered much of their tracks by shaking the snow loose.

He heard a man's voice, close now. Kārlis resisted the instinct to run. He could easily get away from anyone in these woods, but what would be the point with Lileja staggering around drunk.

Sliding behind the tree trunk, he leaned into Lileja. "Get down," he said, lips against her ear.

"Wherss everyone?" she hissed loudly.

"Quiet, Lili," Kārlis said, holding her as they sank to the base of the tree. "Don't move." He opened his coat, wrapping it around her, pressing next to her and the oak. He lowered his hat brim over her head, disguising their shapes, hiding for his life.

As long as there was no dog they might get away. Please God, no dog, Kārlis prayed, too tense to breathe. If there was a dog, life was over.

Light wavered from the other side of the trunk, growing stronger in swings and sweeps. Lanterns or a flashlight, carried by someone come to investigate Lileja's screams.

Whoever it was, Kārlis sensed the intruders were in the clearing now, right on the other side of the tree. He stopped breathing, waiting for them to pass.

"Hold it," said a man. "What's this?"

Kārlis's hope plummeted.

"What?" said a second voice.

"The snow's disturbed here, all over this place," said the first voice, a Russian.

Kārlis held his breath. He imagined the man tracking him to the other side of the tree. At any moment the light would be in his face. Then would he run?

"This is where the assembly was held," the Russian finally said. To Kārlis's relief, the voice was no closer. "Quite a number of them by the looks of it." Then he yelled, "Over here!"

Ak tu kungs, more Cheka? How could they not discover Kārlis and Lileja hiding only meters away?

"I think it was just kids," said the other man in the clearing, a Latvian with deep gravelly voice, probably local militia. "See the swing?"

"I can't see my hand in front of my face," complained the Russian.

They shone light all around, but it only reflected fog's white opacity.

"This swing here," said the Latvian. "It's still swaying."

Lileja shifted. Her body sagged and slumped between Kārlis and the tree trunk.

"What's that?" said the Latvian.

In the silence, Kārlis again imagined the stalkers closing in on him.

"A cigarette butt," the Russian said.

"Who's here?" said a third voice, sounding winded, huffing. It entered the clearing with another beam of light zagging around the surrounding trees.

"Hoodlums," answered the Russian. "And don't say *just kids*. Idealistic punks can be the most dangerous of the citizens," he said, with a note of superiority. "The young tend to be intimately knowledgeable of their locale. And natural liars, too stupid to be afraid. Then they grow up to be worse."

"They went this way," said the new voice.

"I'm not so sure. Look there," said the Latvian. "Anyway, we'll never find them in this fog."

"Maybe not tonight," said the Russian. "But if there're youths like that around town, you need to handle them."

"This swing," the new voice said, "part of the religion, no?"

"Well, folk tradition I suppose, in spring," said the Latvian.

"Old pagan rite, that's what I heard. See that it's destroyed."

"Yah, Comrade."

"Get me a list of the local priests, or whatever you call the religious leaders. And round up their scripture books, whatever they are."

"There aren't religious leaders *per se*," the Latvian said. "The lore's not really written. The *dainas* are sang or recited—"

"Instead of arguing about everything, just bring in the troublemakers," said the Russian. "We have quotas to meet."

"Yah, Comrade. They're mainly grannies, but of course." Assurances became fainter, but the grating, raspy voice promising to round up grandmothers gave Kārlis a chill. The Cheka were hiking away on the same trail they had come.

Kārlis listened hard, following the rustle of clothing and jangle of gear until he could hear nothing more. A hound bayed in the distance. He didn't dare move. What if one of the crafty buggers had stayed behind, and was in the dark clearing now, waiting silently until Kārlis revealed himself? He stayed hidden until his teeth were rattling in his head and his muscles were clumsy from the cold. Finally, Kārlis leaned out to look. The clearing was empty. In the distance, nebulous spheres of light looked far away and small, wobbly in the hands of foreigners to the path.

He tugged Lileja, saying, "Let's go."

She was too weak to stand without aid. He steadied her shivering body. Her breasts felt cushy against him. As his hand pressed the dip of her lower back, Kārlis dared for a moment to feel elated by his good luck. Then Lileja buckled at the waist and vomited all over him.

K. Smiltens, 1975.

- 7 -

Ak gawd! KĀRLIS STOOD, JAW DROPPED IN SHOCK, arms stuck out, chest dripping with hot vomitus. A vile gurgle from Lileja's depths warned him to sidestep just in time to dodge the next projectile stream. He pivoted in panic, searching for the police lanterns, afraid the retching and coughing would draw the Cheka back, but the lights had vanished.

He didn't know how to help Lileja, so Kārlis kept his distance, wiping chunks off his shirt.

She spat and leaned against the pine, wiping her face on her sleeve. "I'm better now," she said, despite her bloodshot eyes, flaccid mouth, and hair plastered to a white cheek.

That's good," Kārlis said, trying not to breathe the sour stink. "We better hurry."

Kārlis opted for a shortcut, handling Lileja like the dangerously volatile, spewing stomach on unsteady legs that she was. The trail was steep at the end, but quickly brought them out of the woods. Kārlis disliked exiting the cover of trees, even though as far as he could see, the village was as dark and lifeless as a cemetery.

He spread the barbed wire as wide as he could and laid down his coat for Lileja, ripping it in the process. Still she snagged her clothing and scratched her arm climbing through. She was in no condition to assist him through the fence. It took him a perilously long time, slithering on his back in the snow, to negotiate the wicked coils of wire. Then, with Kārlis's frozen arm around her waist, they hurried down two short blocks to where a steeply pitched roof edged in icicles marked the sanctuary of the Bier Schtube.

Entering the dimly lit tavern by the back door, Lileja strode urgently upstairs to the family quarters, head bowed. She was filthy with vomit, mud and blood, soaked and freezing. Kārlis was relieved she was going to get cleaned up and wished he could do the same. He'd looked sketchy even before Hugo ground off his face, Lileja threw up on him and barbed wire ripped his coat. The best he could do was walk with head held high.

Surveying the public house thoroughly before entering, Kārlis found the joint empty except for Lileja's father, who sat behind the bar reading a newspaper by light of a desk lamp. Few people would let their guard down by drinking beer under the stern gaze of Josef Stalin, General Secretary of the Communist Party and ruler of the Soviet Union, whose portrait hung behind the bar. Besides, it was after curfew.

Before the occupation, on any given night Kārlis would've seen at least six sets of elbows at the bar and a gang of the usual publicans arguing amiably around the soapstone stove. Now it was so empty he noticed for the first time the pegs on the cedar walls that were usually covered by coats. Without the locals, he saw runes carved on the oak bar, and a geometric folk motif on the woven tablecloths. Wooden beer pitchers were stacked in a pyramid against the wall near a tower of ashtrays—Kārlis had never known the place to have enough of either. The Bier Schtube looked different without the people in it. Or maybe the idea that you might not see a place again made you really look at it.

Mr. Lipkis sniffed and turned a page.

Kārlis arranged his hat and gloves to dry over a chair near the stove and walked to the bar, sliding onto a stool. The day's offerings were scribbled on a slate menu in chalk, the usual misspellings.

"*Sveiks*, Mr. Lipkis," Kārlis said.

Lipkis held out the pages of *Pravda* with a stern expression. "Can you read this?" he asked.

"Some," said Kārlis. He adjusted his glasses and leaned over to look at the bold Cyrillic headlines. "It says something about starving people in the Baltics rejoicing to join the worker's paradise in Russia."

Lipkis nodded, as if that's what he'd thought. "You're lucky," Lipkis said. "You young people learn Russian in school. That's the future. Impossible to learn at my age."

Kārlis had never thought of it that way.

"I understand you've been ordered to report forthwith," the older man said, neatly folding the paper.

"Yah, that's true." Kārlis could easily imagine how the village's sole barkeep already knew he'd been drafted. Probably the man who delivered firewood to the summerhouse had overheard his mother and Tante Agata wailing about the call-up notice. The wood cutter had told the next customer on his delivery route, say the schoolmistress—she loved to blab—who in turn had trotted down to the Bier Schtube and informed

Mr. Lipkis while waiting for her order of smoked eel. Or some such chain of gossip. Kārlis felt oddly warmed to be at the center of the village interest. Even though *talk* was considered a deadly habit, he'd miss these lovable rumormongers.

"Well, if you're old enough to be a soldier, you ought to be old enough to have a beer," Lipkis said, getting up to pull a draught from the tap.

"*Paldies*," Kārlis said, wondering why adults were suddenly plying him with drink. He'd have loved a hot chocolate. He hoped Lileja would be down soon.

"You're welcome," Lipkis said.

"Paldies, *Comrade*," Kārlis added hastily, knowing Lileja's father admired the reigning vernacular. "And I've been admitted to the Art Academy," Kārlis said, reaching for his wallet, carefully as his bruised muscles were getting stiff. Removing the matriculation card, he gave it to Mr. Lipkis with a knowing nod.

"Congratulations," Lipkis said, examining the card and rubbing the stubble on his chin. "But the army's the way to get ahead. Especially given the, uh, the current political landscape."

"I'll go to the Art Academy after the army," Kārlis said.

Lipkis raised his eyebrows. "You can make a good living as a painter," the older man said, gesturing at the portrait of Stalin. "Now that every bar in the country has one of these."

Kārlis knew better than to contradict Lileja's father, but the portrait of Stalin didn't belong in the same conversation as studying at Riga's renowned Art Academy.

"You've heard of socialist realism, right?" Lipkis said. "The style?"

Kārlis wasn't sure.

"That's where the money is," Lipkis said. "It's going to organize the artists. Get them all working along the same theme, so they say." He patted his newspaper like he'd just read about it. "Perfect that style and you'll be heartily rewarded. I'm talking large *dachas* in the country, plenty of work."

Kārlis listened politely, though the hair on the back of his neck was rising.

"Plus, it's the law," Lipkis said, as if detecting Kārlis's doubt.

"It's the law to paint portraits according to a certain style now?"

"Absolutely. That's why the only portrait around here will be Uncle Joe's," Lipkis said, gesturing to the dictator's steely visage.

"But an artist is not just a human camera," Kārlis said. "What about imagination?"

"Foolhardy," Lipkis said. "Draws unwanted attention."

"I want to paint what only *I* can see," Kārlis said. "What's in my head."

"Careful there, son. That's the kind of thinking that makes you a class enemy," Lipkis warned. "Gets you a knock on your door at night."

Lipkis didn't envision his daughter with that kind of thinker, Kārlis guessed. Nor perhaps, with *any* kind of thinker.

Lipkis looked at the matriculation card again. "But you must have potential, to get into the Art Academy. Main thing to watch is the subject matter. Art has to glorify the worker," Lipkis said, wiping away Kārlis's view like a spill on the counter. "You're young. You can adapt. Learn to blend in."

The faint crunch of snow on the walkway outside

drew Lipkis to the window, from where he carefully peered behind the curtain.

Kārlis held his breath.

"NKVD," Lipkis said in a low voice. "Headed toward the train."

The *troika* from the woods, Kārlis thought, ready to bolt.

Shaking his head, Lipkis returned to the bar and folded the newspaper. "Well," he said, "it's getting late."

"I better get going," Kārlis said, standing. "It's just that Lileja said she had something to give me."

"That's right. I'll get it."

Kārlis felt somewhat embarrassed and a little concerned that Mr. Lipkis seemed to know what it was Lileja wanted to give him. Kārlis had assumed Lileja had some intimate forget-me-not for him alone, the departing soldier. A lock of her hair, for instance, tucked in a perfumed handkerchief. A photograph of Lileja, which he would keep near his heart through every foray to the front. Or a beautifully handwritten note, "Hurry Home to Me, Kārlis, My Heart Awaits, Swollen with Affection." He'd been expecting something along those lines. Now, however, when he heard Mr. Lipkis banging his boots on the stairway he realized he was a romantic fool.

Mr. Lipkis stomped back to the bar, red faced. Kārlis recognized the object in his hands, crestfallen. He winced as Lipkis slammed it on the bar. It was the portrait of Lileja at the beach, his masterpiece.

"You got a lot of nerve, boy," Lipkis said, glaring like his eyeballs were about to pop out of his head. "Bringing my daughter home in that condition. First I thought you's just stupid, bringing in this arty crap. But—" Lipkis was right in Kārlis's face, spitting mad. "You got a lot of nerve."

"No, Mr. Lipkis, that wasn't me," Kārlis said. "What happened is—"

Lipkis poked Kārlis hard in the chest, making ribs scream in pain and forcing him to take a step back.

"You got a taste for pain, boy, that's what you got. That and a lot of nerve. Hmmph. Coming in and drinking my beer after what you done to my daughter."

"I didn't do anything, Mr. Lipkis," Kārlis said. "Lileja will tell you."

"She's in no condition to tell anything, you saw to that." Lipkis came within millimeters of Kārlis's face. "Figured you're leaving, what the hell? Never see her again anyway. What the hell!"

"Nothing could be farther— It's not like that—"

"If she is deflowered or in any kind of trouble on account of you, so help me—"

He whacked the portrait against the bar, splintering the wooden frame. "That'll be your skull."

Kārlis backed off, hands up. "She won't be," he said, bumping into a table. "It won't be."

Mr. Lipkis balled his fists and stalked angrily toward him.

"I didn't," Kārlis said, backing toward the door. "I would never—"

"Don't come round here again, boy," Lipkis said. Raising a bulging forearm, his fist coming at Kārlis's belly.

Kārlis crunched in defense as Lipkis connected with the door handle. He banged it open for Kārlis to escape before slamming it shut.

Kārlis stood witless, exposed in the cold night. *Ak tu kungs*, he had not seen that coming. He searched the road for NKVD. Exhaling loudly, he wrapped his arms around his battered ribcage. His hat and gloves were inside warming by the stove. Freezing air staunched what felt like a deep cut inside his chest.

Everything was so *pie joda* messed up.

He turned and limped back toward the woods, yearning to be in his bedroom. Hugo was probably already there, and Kārlis didn't mind. Why had he been so angry with Hugo, anyway? And the draft, suddenly seemed a welcome distraction. Everything was so messed up.

– 8 –

JANIS PĒRKONS SAT AT THE FIREPLACE with his collar unbuttoned and his bowtie dangling around his neck, trying to unwind and hopefully doze off. But his wife managed to jangle his nerves all the way from the kitchen, where she and her aunt clanked a mountain of dinner dishes. Thinking of each person who dined at tonight's table made him sweat, everybody depending on him. How would he continue to feed them all now that his livelihood, or the *means of production* as the Communists liked to call it, had been snatched?

Be grateful you're alive, he reminded himself. For tonight, at least, we have a roof over our heads. Draperies cascaded from the high ceiling to the polished wood floor. Firelight blazed from the hearth. The homey elements wove a powerful illusion of safety. The truth was, at any moment the NKVD might notice the house at the end of the gravel drive flanked by stately linden trees. Then there would be a knock at the door.

The unpleasant thought was interrupted by a thousand jingling bells. His little girl was spinning through the hall making a red skirt swirl in a circle and shaking the coins edging a blue wool shawl. Biruta was wearing her folk costume.

Janis shot out of his chair like a scalded cat, checking that every window was covered. Heart in throat, he brusquely scooped up the silly girl, crazed knowing her innocent play had broken enough laws to incriminate the whole family.

Setting her down by his chair, Janis wanted to shake her.

She looked up at him happily. "It's almost Christmas Eve, Papu!" A gold circlet crossed her forehead. Blond braids hung past her shoulders. She was the picture of northern heritage cherished and handed down for centuries, his little Biruta. Janis tried to calm down.

"Oh, Cookie," Janis began, his heart sinking.

"I always wear my regional dress to church on Christmas Eve."

The fire crackled. A burning log collapsed into itself while Janis contemplated what would no doubt mark the lowest, most miserable moment of his career as father. He lifted her on his lap. "I thought I explained to you there would be no Christmas this year, Cookie. It's forbidden."

"No, Papu." Her jaw went rigid, blue eyes instantly submerged in pools. "You only said Christmas *trees* were outlawed. Now Christmas is against the law too!" A tear streaked down a round cheek. "Why Papu. Why is it bad?"

Because our godless oppressors want to snuff every hope of redemption.

A sickening chill spread over Janis when he thought how the Communists would punish them if the child erred. If she went to school and even mentioned

Christmas, the Cheka might come to the door for the whole family. They'd show no restraint. Neither should he. He had to teach Biruta strict obedience to the Communist master, for her own safety. He'd scare the wits out of her, lock her in her room, take a switch to her backside, that's what he'd do.

No. He shook the thoughts off, knowing he wouldn't do those things. How much time would they even have together? He shook that thought off as well. Unbearable.

In a cold voice, Janis said, "Biruta, if they catch us celebrating Christmas they will hurt Mama and me, put us in jail, and we might not ever see you again."

He watched as fear and shame crumpled her face. He'd hit the mark.

She dissolved in a gush of hot tears at his chest.

Janis hated himself.

"I won't. I won't do it, Papu. Don't worry I won't do it."

"You're a smart girl, Cookie," said Janis, stroking her head. "I know you won't slip up."

The fire needed another log. But Janis wouldn't get up for anything.

"I know how to keep secrets," Biruta said, her voice distorted with the strain of trying not to cry. "I saw Kārlis bury something under the garden gazebo and I haven't told anyone. So you don't have to stop talking when I come in the room. I don't like that. And Papu, I don't like going to Soviet School on Saturdays, to learn Russian. I don't like it. I don't like it." He rocked her quietly until she burst out, "Can we at least have gingerbread?"

Janis sighed in dismay. He admired her unbuckling spirit, but it scared him.

"You drive a hard bargain, Cookie." She was so like

him in that regard. "I think we can manage a secret gingerbread. But the 24th and 25th will be school days same as any other. Don't say the word *Christmas* to anyone. That's important. Don't mention the gingerbread. In fact, don't talk to the other children. You understand? Don't even talk to anyone."

She nodded.

"I won't talk to anybody, Papu."

They watched the fire burn. Then Janis gently bounced Biruta on his knees, extending his hands for her to hold as if they were the reins of a horse. In spite of himself, he whispered the forbidden lyrics of a *daina* they'd always sang together:

Run a little faster, steed of mine
Don't count your steps out one by one
Did I count your oats that way?
No, I gave you purest oats,
Clover reaped on a sunny day.

Tante Agata entered the room with a cup of coffee for Janis.

"Your mother said it's time for bed, little one," she said.

"Papu, I don't like to go to bed," Biruta protested, "because that's when they take people away."

"Where did you get that notion!" Janis said, appalled that the terror gripping the country even penetrated the consciousness of a nine-year-old. "No one will ever take you away, because we have the fastest horse in the country!" He tossed Biruta with a galloping knee-bounce that made her laugh, bells jingling. Beneath his smile he was sick with dread, because if they *wanted* to take her, he'd be powerless to stop them.

Biruta went upstairs whispering, *"Run a little faster, steed of mine…"*

Tante Agata followed her slowly.

"Agata," Janis said from the depths of his chair.

The elderly woman paused on the stairway.

"Better destroy the dress."

Tante Agata nodded, looking weary.

Janis closed his eyes.

When he opened them—he didn't know if it had been a minute or an hour later—his wife was there, putting a leather satchel on the coffee table.

"I've kept my eye out for things coming up for sale, like you told me," Anna said.

He closed his eyes again, sliding heavily back to sleep.

"These should hold their value," Anna said, her voice a fingernail clawing the blackboard of his slumber.

Janis!" She gripped his shoulder, shaking it. "I want you to get an automobile and take us away from here."

Ignore her. She'll go away.

"Janis, what do we do?"

Janis opened his eyes to find his wife sitting on the coffee table, between his knees, leaning toward him.

"Fleeing the country seemed such a drastic measure yesterday," she said, battering him with rapid-fire syllables. "Now I wish we were already gone. Is it too late? I could never go without Kārlis. What if we got him out of the country?"

Janis shifted in his chair, buffering his ears with the cushion.

"What's going to happen next? I don't think I can take any more," she said, whisking the cushion from under his head. "Can you hear me?"

"I hear you." He was awake, the moment of rest obliterated. "I hear you." What he did not hear was any appreciation for the risks he took just to put meat on the table, any gratitude for continually putting the interests of the family before his own safety. Only more demands. "You can't take any more. You want an automobile."

"Yah. Please don't fall asleep."

"I won't. You've seen to that."

"Time is running out. I know it would cost—"

"You have no idea what it would cost, Anna. If you ever stepped foot out of the house you might know how ludicrous, how risky—You have no idea what's out there. I could tell you of an incident just from my lunch hour that would curl your toes. Not to mention the horror of having coffee at the tailor's. Everybody wants something from me. Everyone has their hand out, tugging on my coattails." An unwieldy swell of anger and fatigue overcame Janis. "All I do is work to save our home, but when I'm here and this is all I get from you, I have no home."

Anna stood, turned rigidly toward the mantle and stared at the wall.

That shut her up, Janis thought sourly.

But she didn't cry. The ruffle on her blouse rose and fell with measured breaths, making Janis guess that she was already cried out. What were they even fighting about? He had no idea. She was only voicing something he'd already considered from every angle.

"Can we figure this out tomorrow?" He rose to stand by her. "I am just so dog tired." Leaning an elbow on the mantle, he tried to face her, but she wouldn't look at him. He hated arguing with her. She had the annoying habit of usually being right. "We're on the same side, you and I."

He expelled a deep breath and took his time with the ritual lighting of a cigarette.

"I'm looking at this wrong," Janis finally said. "You ask me for an automobile? I should be highly complimented you think I could get one. Where, Anna, do you suppose I might get a car?"

"Ford Riga, of course."

"Ford Riga was nationalized first thing. What else?"

"Well, there must be other cars…"

"There are about four hundred cars in Riga, Anna. We are not Germany. Though four hundred is a high-water mark for us. Why I remember after the Great War, there were six usable cars in the country. Six! for civilians - and about a hundred for the army. Even the Red Army vehicle fleet is considered poor. You better believe they'd notice something as conspicuous as us driving away in a private auto."

He began to pace in front of the fireplace.

"I have two acquaintances with personal cars. Gentlemen I play cards with, men without families. Their cars were immediately confiscated. Not that it would be impossible to get an auto on the black market, I grant you, for a king's ransom. Then there would be the challenges of getting gasoline, tightly controlled by Russians, and documents for crossing borders, all very expensive, very closely monitored."

He stopped pacing to look at her. Her hair had fallen from its pins and her shoes were off. She looked small.

"But if we got around those issues," Janis said, "Where do you propose we'd go? Where do you imagine is safer than here? You do know what's happening outside that door?" He found himself pointing toward the front door, and lowered his arm, taking a breath. There was no need to badger her. "Do you want to take your chances in the forest with a little girl? Because there'd be no coming back."

He surveyed the room. Four walls had never looked so good.

"My uncle's house in Schwerin," Anna said.

"Ah, Germany. You want to go to the heart of the hornet's nest," Janis said, smoothing his goatee absently. "You do understand *total war*? Meaning *every* resource is applied to the effort. If we were at your uncle's right now, and frankly I wish to God we were, but Kārlis would still have to fight, and maybe me too. Even so, I'd rather be in Germany now. I'd take a predictable nightly bombing by the RAF over guessing what degradation Stalin will fancy next. All of Europe—the whole *kāpost galva* world's at war. We'd have to cross Soviet-occupied Lithuania, Poland, so ravaged, it no longer exists as such. The chances of getting through in a private automobile are slim to nil. Rails are monopolized by the military." His unseeing eyes locked on a section of the baseboard. "It would have to be over the water," Janis concluded, throwing the cigarette butt in the flames.

"None of that would matter if *you wanted* to go," Anna said.

She was right, Janis admitted, feeling both outwitted and buoyed by her confidence in him. What the hell *did* he want anymore? Turned out of Riga. The business gone. Son taken. Putting his arms around her, he pulled her down into the armchair. He wanted it all back.

Anna sat rigidly under his arms, discontent to let him hold her there.

"I wish I could drive away with you this minute, dear lady," Janis said. "But it's not hopeless. We're better situated than many. Maybe we should sit tight, hold the course. Who knows? After the dust settles, maybe the Russians won't be able to maintain their illegal hold on us and they'll go home."

She nodded tentatively, unconvinced.

"We'll prepare options," Janis told her. "We'll prepare for the worst, and look for opportunities. Getting away wouldn't be a simple matter. I'll talk to Rudolfs Zales. He has connections. We'll know what to do when the time comes."

Anna exhaled, shifting in his arms, fitting like the puzzle piece that completed him. Her head under his chin, hair smelling like toasted sugar, her body pressed against his chest; their breathing synchronized for a few measures of solidarity.

"You're so beautiful. Know what you remind me of?" He stroked her hair. "Lustrous. Polished."

"Janis. Stop."

"Beautiful patina."

"Don't you dare compare me to a piece of leather."

"What?" Janis feigned dismay. "It's high praise. Since the dawn of time there's never been a material so flexible for its strength." He zeroed in on her lips trying to kiss her, but she wasn't having it.

"Goodnight, then," Anna said, getting up. "I'm going to sit with Biruta. The child's scared to fall asleep."

Janis felt cold after his wife left. He wanted to follow her upstairs, be in her good graces and get into her eiderdowns. But she was with Biruta and there was much to do and how much time was left was anyone's guess. He put on his coat and went outside through the kitchen door carrying the leather satchel.

The night air was freezing. Locking the door behind him, Janis looked up at the softly lit windows of the second floor bedrooms. Anna was already there, cracking the curtain and peering out. He felt the same way she did, protective of their home. It was a far cry from the poor house where he'd grown up with his widowed mother. But even then, and all the while working his way up from a cobbler, he'd foreseen living in a country manor like this. Nothing ostentatious, there was an understated elegance to the thick stone walls, a charm to the rustic property. But after all, it was just a building and one day the Communists would demand to have it. God let him get his family out before then.

Detecting no one in the vicinity, he set out for his workshop in the old carriage house on the outskirts of the property. He'd let the dirt road become overgrown with weeds to hide the existence of the carriage house from prying eyes. Again checking that he was alone, he ducked into the trees and fumbled his way through the woods in the dark taking care not to create a direct path to the workshop door.

Once inside, he lit lanterns and checked that no light escaped the black window coverings. He fired up the acetylene torch and used it to light the woodstove, kneeling before it for a few warming moments. Turning to the tool closet, he shoved aside garden implements and jiggled the boards of the back wall. The false back lifted out and behind it lay several bulging leather pouches on top of a metal cylinder. He set the pouches aside. The cylinder was heavy, more than half filled with gold and difficult to move. Janis wrested the drum out so he could add his recent black market acquisitions.

He emptied the secret compartments of his boots, gold chains under the fleece lining, gemstones in the hollowed heels. He might have found the skullduggery droll if the consequences of being caught weren't deadly. He removed the pouch worn under his clothes and dumped the contents of the leather satchel procured by his wife, piling treasure on the workbench. Everything was at least 22 karats pure: coins, chains, money clips, handfuls of wedding bands, cigarette boxes, diamond earrings, a ruby studded cross and a filigree tiara encrusted with gems.

As it all went into the cylinder, Janis fantasized about the prospects that would be available on the day he reopened the drum. There would definitely be enough money to fund a leather works, a tried and true enterprise, but what about polymer fabrication, plastics. The field held fascinating possibilities. He'd have the capital to enter it, if strategized correctly. These intervening months—or however long it would be before he could retrieve the cylinder—might be used to plan it out. An exciting possibility, something good might yet come of these wretched circumstances.

Igniting the acetylene torch again, Janis heated the metal surfaces of the drum until molten. He affixed the end cap and hammered delicately until it had an airtight, watertight weld. Using a fine-tipped brush he painted the words, "Property of Janis Pērkons." He put his tools away.

Janis had kept a humidor in his workshop ever since his first promotion to Master Tanner. Extracting a thin cigar, he snipped the end, lit it with the brazing torch and sat puffing, reviewing his handiwork. He considered the leather pouches hidden behind the tool closet to be funds for rapid flight, walking-around money. He eyeballed the thickness of the pouches, making crude estimations of what his family would need: passage to safety, heat, meals, possibly medical aid, and hopefully education. Whereas the cylinder, too heavy to carry, was the mother lode, capital for starting over when this nightmare was over. It required a long-term hiding place.

Turning off his work lights he stepped outside

cautiously, looking to see if anyone was around. In the foggy nighttime solitude, Janis ambled over the property considering where to stash the drum.

The beauty of his homeland never failed to charm him. From the mossy bracken of the forest floor to the emerald flames of the northern lights, Janis reckoned this was the most wonderful place on earth. The thought of leaving it broke his heart, but Latvia was not the country he loved as long as the Communists were in charge. He paused to consider the oddity of a multi-trunked linden tree rising darkly against the fog. Then he stubbed out his cigar and strode over to the well for a drink of cold water straight from the bucket.

- 9 -

ERIKS GAILIS LEANED TOWARD THE FIRE, rubbing his shoulder and cursing the unyielding nature of frozen earth. He sat on a tree stump, one in a ring under a blackened chimney flue suspended from the high rafters of a stone barn that housed fifty cows. Steam issued from an iron kettle hanging from a tripod. That and a nearby box of dishes gave Eriks the impression something was about to be brewed. At least, he hoped so.

"Arm hurt?" Kristaps asked, unwinding strips of cloth from his feet and drying them near the flame.

"I'm just thankful I *have* arms after jumping off a moving train," Eriks said.

"And a tongue," Kristaps said, with a knowing air that was troubling.

"How 'bout a little advance notice next time risking limbs is called for?" Eriks said, as Caleb sat down nearby.

"Less time to fuss this way," Caleb said. "I could see you were a natural, mate. You roll like a wheel."

"Damned irresponsible," Eriks muttered. "Could've broken my neck."

Thinking he saw Caleb and Kristaps pass an amused look, he sighed heavily.

Eriks had already adapted to the stench that had bowled him over upon arrival to the barn, eagerly hailing the stinky enterprise as a haven of warmth and safety. The sun had barely risen, but a crew of boys already hummed along with pails and stools, tossing hay, squirting milk and shoveling manure among an infinite line of swishing cow tails. Eriks was impressed by the discipline and rhythm of the place, especially since most of the boys looked younger than him.

"So," Caleb said, suppressing a yawn, "everyone does chores here. We rotate. Shoveling muck is an easy way to start if you want."

Caleb got up and ambled toward the back of the barn, where ladders rose to the hayloft.

"Are you pitching hay?" Eriks asked.

"I'm sleeping in the hay," Caleb said. "My chores happen at night. Like I said before, you can help me and Kristaps if you have the stomach for it. But I warn you, some of the stuff we have to do... well, it's damned irresponsible."

"I'll go with you," Eriks said, automatically.

Caleb saluted him. "Then I'll see you tonight."

A chubby-faced youngster whizzed by, running for the barn door. Before Eriks could call out, "Where's the fire?" another boy ran past, and a third.

Eriks raised his eyebrows at Kristaps.

"They just want to carry the grub for the *Princese*," Kristaps said. "She's about to make her morning appearance at the kitchen door."

"*Princese?*"

"Hmm. Old Farmer Baron's grand-daughter or grand-niece or such."

"Wait, I know who you mean," Eriks said. "Is her name Zelma?"

"Maybe."

"Dark hair? Pretty, in a librarian kind of way?"

"Prettiest girl around here," Kristaps said, glancing up and down the row of cows.

"I have a message to deliver to Zelma Barons," Eriks said, rubbing his hair back and straightening his clothes. "She's a friend of mine from school." Checking his pocket, Eriks found the envelope Mr. Barons had told him to give his daughter. "You say she's in the kitchen, in that wooden farmhouse?"

"Is most mornings," Kristaps said.

Before striking out to meet Zelma, Eriks grabbed some stalks of fresh straw, twisted them into a loop and poked it into his lapel buttonhole. He stepped from the barn into a stinging cold morning and followed the tracks in the snow across the dairy compound.

The smitten farmyard urchins were already gathered at the kitchen door, elbowing one another off the stoop. When the top half of a Dutch door opened, Eriks understood why they vied for position, craning necks for a look inside. It was a window into a world of warm yellow light, fragrant with roasted oats. Framed by the gray-grained wood, was Zelma. Even layers of wool sweaters and work overalls couldn't disguise her curvy figure. A sweep of hair escaped her cap, dark against a long creamy neck.

Zelma handed mitts to two boys before opening the lower door.

"Careful not to spill," she said, as they carried a heavy kettle out between them. She gave a basket to the third boy. It looked heavy with jars of something, covered with a towel. Watching them leave, Zelma saw Eriks. Her eyes sparked with immediate recognition.

"You're here," she whispered, resting her gaze on him. "That can't be good."

Eriks shook his head, not trusting his voice. For some reason, Zelma's sympathy tugged loose control of his chest, making him want to pour his fears into her bosom and cry his eyes out. Instead he said, "I have a message for you. From your father."

She sucked in her breath. "What about?" Her hands shook when she grabbed the envelope, stuffing it into a pocket. "What?" she demanded, eyes wide.

"Nothing. They're fine. I saw them this morning. They're okay."

Pans clattered in the kitchen, making Zelma look nervously over her shoulder.

"Just a minute, for the bread," Zelma said, reverting to a public, businesslike tone. She turned into the kitchen and, watching her walk to the oven, Eriks saw a man in there looking around with a clipboard in his hand. He wore an olive green, wool uniform with tall black boots, and took an immediate interest in Eriks.

The two held eyes for a prickly moment. Eriks couldn't avoid it, but he instantly regretted being seen. He stood out like a cleaver among butter knives. He was taller than the official and, like Caleb had recently pointed out, guilty of being fighting age.

Zelma returned and blocked the man's view by pushing an armful of warm loaves to Eriks.

"They're collectivizing the farm," she whispered. "Tell Caleb, tonight's delivery will have to be the last." Zelma looked up at him. He saw her breath in the rise and fall of her sweater. "My room is on the second floor," she said. "The north-east corner."

"What do I look like, a squirrel that I can walk up the side of the building?" Eriks asked Caleb in the privacy of the hayloft. "Because that was clearly an invitation."

"She said *tonight*," Caleb clarified, agitated by the other aspects of Zelma's message. "Tonight's the last drop. So this is happening *now*. Christ Almighty."

Eriks examined the ladder he'd just climbed. Notches kept it from slipping, but it wasn't permanently attached to the loft. "Sometimes the simplest solution is the most obvious," Eriks said under his breath, wondering what Zelma wore beneath those farmer coveralls.

Caleb looked over. "If you think access to the *princese's* boudoir is your problem, mate, then you're not grasping the situation."

"Actually I don't think access will be a problem."

"We can no longer stay here," Caleb said, looking at the surrounding mounds of dry straw like it was the Taj Mahal. "I've seen plenty of farms collectivized. The place'll be crawling with Russians. There will be nowhere to hide. Not even under your girlfriend's skirts. They list all the equipment including every person working here. Then the state redistributes it all, to make it all so much more efficient. God help us. And if you don't want to be redistributed too, mate, and by the way I have no intention of being picked up, then we better be gone." Caleb sniffed and gave Eriks an accusatory glare, as if he knew Eriks was thinking about the strand of dark hair that had slipped from

Zelma's cap. "Hey, this concerns you," Caleb said. "I guarantee after you spend a night in a frozen rail yard, trying to sleep, trying to hide, you'll take an interest in this."

"Okay, okay. What do you want from me?"

"I don't know. If we could find a small, family farm the Russians don't want. Maybe sleep in the barn in exchange for smuggling. That's the usual deal. But the Ivan's are onto every speck of dirt now. Damned if there's a *kulak* left in this country, but we've got to find one now. Kristaps has no *kāpost galva* shoes. How's he going to keep up?"

"Well, these fellows we're taking the food to," Eriks said, sobered. "How do they survive in the woods without freezing?"

Caleb gave him a withering look. "They are the Forest Brotherhood. They have their ways and connections. I don't know what they are. All I know is, they exist to fight and if you don't have a weapon they got no use for you."

There could be any number of reasons why a fellow might be climbing a ladder into the farmhouse after breakfast, Eriks thought, as he ascended the northeast corner. If he got caught, he would feign knocking icicles off the storm drain or rescuing a kitten. He was more worried about what to say to Zelma, if she was even there. What if he'd completely mistook her cryptic remark? Looking at this in the clear morning light, how could he possibly construe what she'd said as a proposition? At school she'd been a boring, goody two-shoes. Why suddenly the seductress? Was it a trap?

The curtains were tightly shut, so Eriks had to slide the window open to see inside Zelma's room. It was unlocked. Someone was expecting him. He prayed it would be the creamy-necked vixen and not Comrade Green Wool. Parting her draperies, he took a long look. Then he pushed his head through and climbed in.

The room was dim. Zelma was sitting on the side of the bed, her hair loose. She turned her head when Eriks came in, but then returned to staring forward, as if she wanted to finish her thought before dealing with him showing up. It gave Eriks a moment to take her in. Her figure was covered from neck to ankle by light blue underwear. The soft fabric formed a Y on her lap, where the crease of her thighs met the line of her legs. Socked feet just reached the floor. Cold air from the open window had aroused her nipples. Eriks closed the window and rubbed some warmth into his hands. She looked up and he recognized a loneliness in her eyes that matched how he'd been feeling. Maybe holding her would save them both.

The bedsprings squeaked when Eriks sat hesitantly next to her. He had no idea what to say. To his relief, Zelma moved right into his arms. He kissed her on the lips. To his amazement, her fingers scrabbled at the buttons of his shirt. His skin stung with cold air where she pushed his thermal over his head. When her fingers fumbled at his belt buckle, he thought he'd burst right in his trousers knowing she was going to touch him. He dove under the blankets, naked, pulling her onto him. By the time he'd helped her wriggle out of her winter underwear, a warm space enveloped their bodies. The unsolvable problems were forgotten, none as urgent as this single, hot connection. A moan escaped Zelma's lips as Eriks entered the only place where his worries couldn't follow. Traitorous bed springs squealed like an alarm for the authorities. Eriks spurned them in pursuit of a grand, messy delirium that blew away all caution. Afterward, there were scant moments to hold one another before paranoia crawled into bed with them.

"You ever have the feeling something swift and terrible is about to happen to you," Eriks whispered, lacing his shoes and watching Zelma pull her coveralls back in place.

"You're just now getting that feeling?" Zelma asked. "Something swift and terrible has already happened to us."

"I had you wrongly pegged as a frightened little bird," he said, admiring her dark locks before she hid them under her cap.

"I had you pegged as an arrogant, reckless playboy."

Eriks waited for her to say that now she believed differently. In the silence, unfamiliar noises in the building made his mouth dry with anxiety. "I mean you don't normally seduce fugitives. Do you?"

"There's no normal anymore," Zelma said.

"Well, I think you're inordinately brave," Eriks said, feeling both swirly and serious. "Noble, even."

"Why? For having a roll with you?"

"Yah. For following your heart despite lurking farm collectivizors," Eriks said. He pointed to the wall as if they both knew someone in green wool with a clipboard skulked on the other side. "I'm glad you weren't too afraid."

Zelma looked amused. "You're taking my mind off the scary stuff."

"Really. What frightens you, my pretty little sandwich," Eriks said, wrapping his arms around her.

"First of all, you calling me a sandwich has me a little worried. But mainly, since you ask, today I have to go pick up supplies at this sinister village, Patikamspils. You know it?"

"No. But I saw a sign for it from the train."

"Picturesque little hamlet, scary as hell. Going there's like getting caught in a spider web."

"How so?" Eriks said, sliding his hand under Zelma's sweater.

Zelma looked down toward his hand with a tolerant expression before continuing. "It's home to the most rabid militia you never want to meet," she said. "They love making examples of errant townspeople. I have to drive the sledge right past NKVD command center, this old manor house where they're all lounging around, waiting for someone to punish."

"Well, can't you take a different route? There must be a back road."

"Nay. In winter there's only the one narrow road in and out, through deep forest. It's the only one cleared of snow. And it's edged with tall, frozen berms, so once I turn down it, I can't turn around."

Eriks nodded. "A trap." He could visualize the situation.

"That's only half of it," Zelma said, lowering her voice. "The folks living there are the worst sort of Soviet collaborators, the biggest turncoats in the country. Ready to tattle on their own mother to get in good with the Ivans."

Shaking her head, Zelma suddenly pressed her hand to her face, looking conscience-stricken. "Last time I went, I took this boy, Daniels. He accidentally broke a glass in the pub. One of the villagers got up from his beer and ran down the road, nearly two kilometers, to tell the Cheka. Trying to win favor, you know, saying something like an anti-Soviet youth was badgering the village, and that it would be easy to capture him."

"And did they?"

"Oh, yah! In a jiffy! Not just one or two guys, either. The whole kāpost galva outpost was raging. And guns! They came ready to take on an army."

"I'll go with you," Eriks said, retracting his hand from Zelma's sweater and smoothing her hair. "I'll take your mind off the scary stuff. Yah?" Eriks wanted to succeed where this Daniels fellow, whoever he was, had failed.

"Oh, no. I go by myself now. Keep my head down. You'd just make matters worse. They'd view you and your fancy coat as an invitation to trouble." Flashing a mischievous smile, she added, "Like I did."

Eriks felt somewhat invincible as he climbed back out the window. He leaped past the lower ladder rungs into the snow and rolled up like he'd just returned from vacation. The ladder felt light as balsa wood as he carried it back to the hayloft. Climbing up, he curled in a sun-warmed corner and slept hard, arms around a bag of oats. Hoping to conjure dreams of Zelma, instead sleep was haunted by Comrade Green Wool.

He awoke with a jerk, not knowing where he was, someone shouting. Eriks rolled over, eyes adjusting to the dark as he prepared to scramble under the straw. When a madcap peal of laughter split the air, he relaxed. Just Kristaps. Eriks got up slowly, rubbing his stiff shoulder and peering from behind a rolled bale of hay. Caleb and Kristaps were on the other side, lit by a candle in a pail, wrestling in the straw like fools.

"Stop tickling me or I'm gonna pee!" Kristaps yelled, squirming away from Caleb and springing to his feet. Caleb jumped up too, pushing his sleeves up to the elbow, and the two circled each other in boxer stances.

Eriks shook his head, once again heartened by

their mettle. Stretching, he brushed straw off his coat. The barn below was dark, except for glowing orange embers at the fire ring. The cows had been released from their milking lineup and were milling freely in sociable clumps, stamping hooves, chewing cud and farting contentedly. Eriks envied them their situation. Outside, twilight was falling with the heavy fact that he had to leave the dairy before an armed man in green wool reduced him to a tally on a clipboard.

He wondered if Zelma had made it back from her errand, if he dared to look for her in her room to say goodbye. He'd never known a girl he wanted to take home to meet his parents. Now that he had, home and parents were gone. What if he never saw Zelma again, either?

On the other side of the hay bale, Caleb and Kristaps were spoofing a fistfight. Caleb punched wildly at Kristaps, shouting, "Take that you little runt!" The kid reacted with head snaps and theatrical grunts.

Grateful for the entertainment, Eriks stepped from the shadows.

Kristaps screamed.

"Shit!" Caleb said, flinching.

They were staring at Eriks as if Stalin himself had materialized from the gloom.

"What's wrong with you!" Caleb said, sharply.

"What'd I do?" Eriks said, as startled as they were. Then he burst out laughing. "Hoo! You suckers a little edgy?" His belly shook with mirth. "You should've seen the look on your faces!"

"You can't just appear from the shadows all creepy like that," Kristaps said.

"Not funny, mate," Caleb reproached. "Gave me a kāpost galva heart attack."

"Ah, that was grand," Eriks said, sighing and feeling human. He hunched his shoulders and popped his head up, mocking Caleb's look of fright.

"Oh, yah?" Caleb said. He grabbed Eriks by the collar and threw some swings at him, stopping his fist miles away. "That's for scaring the cabbage out of me and—"

"Looks so phony," Eriks critiqued. "If you're giving out a pummeling, make it believable at least. Like this. Here." Eriks pushed Kristaps into Caleb. "Hold him down."

Kristaps pretended to struggle as Caleb pinned his arms back.

"You both stay hidden behind my body, see?" Eriks said, pulling his fist high. "Lean in tight, Kristaps. Yah? Caleb, make these hidden palm-punches, hear that?"

The two caught on right away.

"I telegraph my punch. Kristaps, you— no, wait half a second. Now jerk your head." They got into a jaw-busting groove with convincing sound effects.

"Keep your arms back!" Eriks told Kristaps.

Kristaps's eyes, looking over Eriks's shoulder, suddenly widened for real.

Eriks's heart raced. Someone was behind him.

"Hey!" said a voice.

His fist high, Eriks whipped around, every nerve unhinged and raw, heart trilling in a drum roll. *Phew!* Zelma was standing on the upper rungs of the ladder, leaning forward on slender arms. He could barely collect his wits.

"*Sveiks, cilvēks,*" she said. "Sorry to scare you."

"Hey, Princese," Caleb said, coolly pushing Kristaps off him.

Eriks went over to the ladder and reached for her

hand, hoping she wouldn't notice he was shaking.

"You've brought the expected air of sophistication to the place," Zelma said as he pulled her onto the loft.

Eriks could only grin foolishly and reluctantly release his grip on her.

"I found snowshoes," Zelma told Caleb, in a low voice. "The bags are packed, outside the kitchen door. And, since it's the last time, they're heavy."

"Wonderful," Caleb said, with characteristic finesse toward daunting tasks. To Kristaps, "Let's go get them."

He and Kristaps climbed down the ladder, leaving Eriks and Zelma alone together in the loft.

Eriks felt lightheaded, the singing in his groin leaving not a drop of blood in his brain. "Come here," he said, quickly. "I want to show you something."

He led her behind rolled bales of straw, taking small steps in the dim light to the back wall. There, a wooden shutter as big as a tractor covered the window opening, secured by a cross bar. Eriks lifted the bar out and one side of the shutter swung open. A freezing torrent of air blasted them. They melded together on their perch thirty feet up, dwarfed by a view of a gray frozen universe.

It seemed they were on the same level as the evening star. Below them, fencing outlined the dairy's property, poking up from the moonlit snow in a dashed line. The cleared easement that was the railroad tracks could be seen farther out, but beyond that... Eriks gulped. The forest loomed to the farthest outreaches of the horizon in a colorless palette of smudged lines that looked unforgiving and deceptively peaceful.

She gasped at the sight.

Eriks pulled Zelma tight, shivering to the marrow of his bones. Somewhere in that vast warren of trees, people were defying the Russians and surviving on their own terms. Tonight, he'd wend a path, under Caleb's guidance, to meet them.

"You know how dangerous it is to work with Caleb?" Zelma asked. "What they do to you if you get caught? Because sometimes you act like this is all fun and games."

In answer he held her tighter.

-10-

IT WAS DARK BY THE TIME ERIKS CAUGHT UP with Caleb and Kristaps outside the kitchen door, no moon in sight. A pair of snowshoes, wood-framed with criss-crossing rawhide laces, was lying next to lumpy, stuffed burlap bags. Eriks strapped the contraptions over his city shoes and stood up, feeling empowered. He'd stay drier now, floating over the surface of the snow instead of post-holing with every step. But hoisting the heavy bag over his shoulder did make him sink lower in the snow and he had to lift his feet high as he trudged after Caleb into the trees.

The bag emitted an arousing odor. Blood? Perhaps it held freshly butchered chickens. It took every ounce of restraint he could muster not to rip into the stores. But his prospects depended on gaining the favor of whoever got these picnics. He was nervous about his appointment with the Forest Brotherhood and determined to impress them with his chicken-delivering acumen. Nevertheless, his stomach complained in a way he'd never before known. Ignoring it made him angry.

Several meters into the trees, Caleb stopped and loaded his sack into some sort of feed trough turned drag sled. It was already stuffed with the other bags and loaded with hay, probably for a horse. Kristaps sat on top of the heap, smoking.

"I can tell you from experience," Caleb said, giving Eriks one side of a leather harnass, "that it'll be fastest overall if you and I pull the sleigh." Caleb positioned the strap against his shoulder, ready to put his back into the effort.

"What?" Eriks said. "We're the mules and Kristaps rides up top like a sultan on a magic carpet?"

Kristaps looked down at Eriks, blowing a smoke ring.

Eriks noted the cardboard-wrapped feet perched against the provisions and acknowledged this division of labor was probably reasonable. But he was grumpy about it anyway.

Caleb did not appear concerned with Eriks's opinion, looking furtively in all directions and tugging the tub-travois until it started to slide across the trackless snow.

Eriks had no choice but to keep up with his side. He tried several uncomfortable strap-against-shoulder positions before catching traction and making any progress. He had never done anything so brutish in his life. Fear that a farm collectivizor or other authority might confront him whirred in his head like a flickering horror film.

They had just arrived at the dairy fence when Kristaps said, "Whoa, hold it right here." He jumped off the rig and scampered like a forest creature, disappearing into the trees.

"Where's the fool going?" Eriks demanded, toes already aching-numb and aggravated at standing still.

He shot Caleb a look of annoyance. "Let's keep moving. Obviously he can keep up if he wants to."

Caleb was tolerant. "Wait a minute," he said, looking into the trees where Kristaps had disappeared.

Yoked to Caleb, Eriks could not make a move they didn't both agree on. So he waited, fuming. The moon was rising by the time he finally saw the clumsy whelp coming through the trees carrying something unwieldy. Eriks could've strangled Kristaps.

"Couldn't find where I put it," Kristaps said, coming up to the sled out of breath. He was dragging a pickax that he must've stashed earlier in the day.

He hoisted it on top of the burlap bags and climbed back aboard.

Eriks tugged on the harness, grimacing at the added weight. "This is *kāpost galva* heavy," he said. "Why add that?"

"Seems good," was all Kristaps could say.

"Oh, sure. I bet it seems great from your point of view, riding up top. I mean, it would be splendid to arrive with a gasoline-powered generator and a ripsaw, but since you aren't the one dragging this *kāpost galva* tub, don't go adding unnecessary weight to the deal." Eriks felt strangely monstrous. "And you stole a pickax from Farmer Barons? After he stuck his neck out sheltering us in his dairy?"

"Actually *the People* stole everything from Farmer Barons," Kristaps said, climbing onto the trough-sled and settling in. "I stole from the People."

"Good thinking," Caleb said.

"Well, if you're so smart, why didn't you get one for everyone?" Eriks said, now angry for sounding like an ass.

Kristaps spread his hands.

Caleb said, "We'll hafta share, mate."

"Yah, fine. I'm just the mule." Eriks didn't know what angered him more, the extra weight, that he would show up to the rebel meeting empty-handed, or that he felt powerless to stop his spirit's downward spiral.

"Here," Caleb said, opening a burlap bag and reaching an arm inside. He pulled out a cold, baked potato and gave it to Eriks.

Eriks crammed so much potato into his mouth he could hardly chew. He knew he was going to feel better now, though disheartened at how quickly he'd crumbled facing adversity. A pinch of snow slaked his thirst. He wanted to cry at what lay ahead.

It was one thing to learn in school that Latvia was forty-seven percent wooded plains. It was quite another to plod past every single pine, spruce and birch in the country, which is how the endless hike through frozen forest felt to Eriks. Steering the heavy tub between densely spaced trees and sharp twiggy thickets was a constant, inefficient, slow-going tug-and-push. Moonlight streaked branch-shadows on the snow underfoot. But through the trees, Eriks glimpsed the bright glow of the moon reflecting off what looked like an easily traversed open meadow or possibly a frozen pond.

"Why don't we cut across that?" Eriks asked, pointing his stick.

He'd quickly learned the value of a stick. Essential for pushing icy branches aside, the stick banged snow off low-hanging evergreens before Eriks passed underneath, and knocked off the sludge that kept accumulating on top of his snowshoes.

"Nay, Stupid," Kristaps said, from the sled. "Tracks."

"Lead the NKVD straight to Silent Forest," Caleb said. "They'd have our heads."

It wasn't clear to Eriks who would have their heads, the secret police or the renegades hiding in these woods. Either threat seemed remote compared to the certainty of losing toes if he didn't warm up soon.

"You give them too much credit," Eriks said, also not bothering to clarify the pronoun. He wiped his nose on an icy sleeve. "Nobody in his right mind would be out here in this weather, much less looking for tracks."

"Never said anybody was in his right mind," Caleb muttered, the words distorted, spoken from a quivering chin.

Eriks could see newspaper sticking out of Caleb's cuffs and collar. He'd probably employed this practical heat-keeping measure while Eriks had been busy making Zelma swoon. Eriks staggered forward with muscles of jelly, saying, "I should've salted my *apakšbikses*. I'm frozen stiff. Ha!"

"For once I don't mind your *hot air*," Caleb said.

"Are we almost there?" Eriks asked for the hundredth time.

Caleb sank back onto his heels looking upward, as if to study the big picture. Then he pushed forward.

"Please don't tell me we're lost," Eriks said.

"Can't you shut up?" Kristaps said in the hunted, bossy tone he'd used when Eriks first met him on the train. "They're out there."

"You always have to dwell on that?" said Eriks.

Kristaps said, "Everyone hates me because I'm paranoid."

Eriks answered with a defiant clack of the stick to his snowshoe and plodded forward. For a moment it was quiet enough to hear ice crystals crunching underfoot. Searching the dark, unnerving curtain of tree trunks made Eriks's chest feel like a tight shirt ready to rip. "The thing of it is," he gasped. "For every step we take deeper into these woods, we'll have to take a matching step to get us back out. Have you considered that?" He tried and failed to be calm and think of something funny. "If we don't find somewhere warm to hole up and—"

A wind rose up, shaking the twiggy treetops like a matchbox.

"Wait. I just caught a whiff of wood smoke," Eriks said. "Did you smell that?" He tipped up his nose, but the scent had vanished.

Caleb, paying him no attention, suddenly stopped. He glanced at Kristaps as if for confirmation, then turned the loaded trough toward a small knoll. The space between tree trunks was cramped. They had to push through the underbrush single-file, with Eriks removing his harness and dropping to the rear, head down to avoid eye-poking branches.

"Hold it here," Caleb whispered, gesturing for them to halt without turning his head.

Eriks waited.

Kristaps slid off the vehicle, and stood behind Caleb's elbow, pickax in hand, peering ahead.

Eriks strained to see over their shoulders into the woods, when something like a broomstick poked him in the back. Without looking, he pushed it away with a gloved hand, but it returned with a jab to his kidney. Suddenly Eriks knew, what he'd taken to be a branch was the barrel of a rifle. Someone was pushing a gun into his back. A roar filled his ears despite the silent forest, and his hands went numb. He felt strangely tranquil, detached, wondering if the gun were loaded.

"In dense woods..." intoned the man behind him.

The words made no sense, compounding confusion.

Steel pushed into Eriks's coat.

His brain froze. He saw his hands held empty in the air before him.

A metallic click sent his body shaking, teeth clattering in his skull.

"...the trees grow straight," Caleb supplied in a clear voice, stepping around from the front of the sled and approaching whomever stood at Eriks's back. "The trees grow straight."

After a lag, the pressure, it seemed reluctantly, left Eriks's back.

"Hell, Caleb," said the voice, suddenly genial. "Heard you yapping an hour ago. Who's the loudmouth?"

Eriks turned around, still trembling.

A man in white camo fatigues was lowering his rifle with a deliberate, measured movement. Eriks had no doubt the gunman would've blasted soul-from-body according to protocol had Caleb not stepped up at that precise instant with ... what, some sort of pass code.

Burning at the callousness of it, Eriks only listened with one ear as Caleb explained to the gunman, calling him Aivars, about the dairy being collectivized. While they made mouth noises about exactly how many Russians had overrun the farm and the strength of their hardware, Eriks's eyes wandered from the partisan's assault rifle up to the black wool tam worn low on his forehead. It was studded with hammer-and-sickle NKVD cap badges that glinted dull red in the moonlight.

"Barons sent him," Caleb said, nodding toward

Eriks. "He's a bona fide."

Aivars studied Eriks through narrowed eyes.

Head buzzing, Eriks only then noticed that two other men stood behind Aivars. One was portly, wearing a black beanie and a white cape fashioned from a mattress cover, over a black turtleneck sweater. The two-toned get-up reminded Eriks of the national bird, the White Wagtail.

"Tell Glamour Boy to keep his trap shut next time," Wagtail said.

It steamed Eriks to be talked over like that, rather than directly addressed. He'd get common courtesy, he reckoned, if he too were holding a gun. Without one, he was not even a person.

Behind Wagtail stood a tall, thin man, whose stick figure was accentuated by a black frock coat. Sun-leathered skin stretched over his bony face. The brim of a homburg hid his eyes. Slinging his rifle behind his shoulder, the black stick figure strode to the sleigh, where he dumped the contents of a burlap bag.

Eriks stared stupidly as rifles clattered out amid some rolling potatoes. He'd not known they were smuggling arms.

The thin man plucked a potato in long, twig fingers and tossed it to Wagtail. Then he gave one to Aivars.

An owl hooted as the men ate.

Eriks salivated, acid eating his stomach lining. Caleb and Kristaps didn't ask for food, so neither did he, but he was *kāpost galva* livid to not be included in the meal.

"What you staring at, Glamour Boy?" Aivars said, mouth full.

"Nothing," Eriks said. "If I blink my eyes will freeze shut."

"Hoo-tah!" Aivars crowed and looked at the thin

man. "Haralds, you hear that? Glamour Boy is a wit!"

"This rifle has no stock," the man called Haralds said, examining the arms. "And here's one without a sight."

"The usual obsolete scavengings," said Aivars.

"Might make one usable weapon if we put them all together, but if you're thinking these will admit you to the party," Haralds said, "then you are mistaken."

"Couldn't hassle my granny with this arsenal," said Aivars, pushing items around. "Pickax looks good, though."

"That's mine," Kristaps said, with a white-knuckle grip on the pickax. Eriks was impressed with the kid's brass. His cardboard-wrapped feet were not visible, but they must've been blocks of ice by now.

"Is that so?" Aivars said, raising his eyebrows at Kristaps. "In that case, you might have a job, little Bee-in-your-Cap."

"Damn few bullets," said Haralds, searching the bags. "Are there more where these came from?"

"It wasn't easy getting even these," Caleb said.

"Did you contact those names I gave you?"

"Found the chemist and a few others. But people are disappearing, or don't want to be found. Here," Caleb said, extracting a pouch from his jacket. "Here's the collection."

"Next time spend it," Haralds said, loosening the drawstring pouch for an unimpressed look inside. "Cannot buy powder in these woods. You get a line on some morphine? Penicillin? Vodka?"

"Some. But like I said, we had to clear out of there," Caleb said. "And we can't go back."

"More to the point," interrupted Wagtail, "nobody will be arriving with anything better in this forest tonight. So let's get going with what we got."

"Let's get organized!" Aivars chimed, with queer enthusiasm.

Wagtail and Haralds assumed the lead, muscling the makeshift sledge through the trees with the energy of fresh horses. Caleb and Kristaps pushed from behind. Eriks, defrocked of the harness and suddenly light, stumbled along behind uninvited, hoping that the guerrillas' clean-shaven faces meant the proximity of hot water.

Under the high moon, branches cast black webs on the snow.

Eriks rubbed his shoulders, sore from pushing against the harness. He followed Kristaps down the bank of a creek, clutching ropey willow fronds for balance. Wagtail, Haralds and Caleb maneuvered the sled up the opposite bank without difficulty. There the trail widened and traversed a glen.

"Knock. Knock."

Eriks was dismayed to find Aivars walking at his shoulder. He hadn't forgiven the man for pointing a gun at him.

"The sheep have called," Aivars said, leaning into Eriks's face. "They want the fancy coat back."

Eriks stiffened, not enjoying the joke.

Aivars chuckled. "Just kidding. What's your story?"

Eriks's story had always begun with his family owning Riga's finest department store. But here in the woods, his pedigree was not only irrelevant, he was sure Aivars would somehow use the information to torment him. He paused walking to think. His personal decline had begun three days ago, when he'd crossed Igor Volkov.

"Communists installed this apparatchik in the neighborhood," Eriks said, still not sure how events were related. "Then everything went to hell."

"A high-level party player?" Aivars asked, standing in Eriks's path and looking keen.

"Nay. Just my age," Eriks said, stopping and recalling with disgust the memory of Volkov's heart-shaped face. "Some beginner bureaucrat."

"A colonist," Aivars said. "Starting a career and working his way up the ladder."

"Yah. Same day I laid eyes on Igor Volkov, one friend was dragged to the Corner House, another was beat to a bloody pulp, my parents were *picked up*," Eriks was becoming anesthetized to the new reality. "The Cheka came back for me, so I ran." He knew better than to try to impress someone of Aivars's experience with the story about the NKVD shooting at him. "It's been an absolute string of disasters."

"I like the way you put it," Aivars said, looking concerned. "It *has* been a kāpost galva *string of disasters* ever since those Russian tanks rolled into Town Square." Aivars held his Mosin-Nagant with an unnerving, twitchy two-handed readiness, upper body taut under the white-gray fatigues.

"How do I find out what happened to my parents?" Eriks asked, suddenly aware he could learn much from Aivars.

"You don't want to find out, Glamour Boy," Aivars said, in a sympathetic tone. "Trust me. Don't invite the specters in," he tapped at his head. "They don't leave." He sidled close to Eriks, as if sharing a confidence. "They took *my* family." Aivars swung his head toward Eriks to display the NKVD cap badges lined across his beret. "This *kāpost galva*," he said, fingering the first hammer-and-sickle in the row, "took revenge on my wife." He pointed to each of three trophies. "My son, Rainis. And little Inga."

Sweat dotted Eriks's brow and turned to frost.

Aivars said, "I sent them Russian bastards to the Shade Mother." Suddenly he whipped around and fired his rifle into the trees, hand married to the bolt action. *Bam, bam, bam.* "*Kāpost galvas!*" he shouted, into the echoing reports. "That's your *kāpost galva* ass, *kāpost galva!*"

Eriks stood frozen to the earth, electrified as bullets tore the forest air.

Aivars fired another round. "You picked a fight with me," he screamed. "I'm not a fighter, *kāpost galva*. I'm a killer."

Eriks's sensorium rocketed. Eardrums rang, pulse jackhammered in his neck, tongue tasted gun smoke. He suddenly felt eyes watching him. They'd been there all along, the hateful eyes of those who despised Aivars even more than Eriks did for aiming at them, aiming to kill. He turned with dread, wishing he were invisible.

The other Forest Brethren had not stopped for the spectacle. The glow of Wagtail's mattress-pad cape bobbed and glided through a tunnel of tree limbs, growing smaller. Haralds, stickish in his long black coat, looked like a marching tree shadow. They were pushing the trough up a narrow trail and would soon be out of sight. With a heaving breath, Eriks tried to catch up in awkward high-lift snowshoe steps, anything to avoid being alone with Aivars.

But Aivars kept up easily. "You seem like a nice fella, Glamour Boy," he said, speaking again in the genial voice. "The nicer the boy, the bigger his heart, the more he feels, the bigger killer he can become."

Eriks cringed. Cold seared his bulging eyes. Aivars was insane. Killers were criminals and he was in the presence of one.

"The person who's lost the most is the best killer," Aivars explained.

Eriks didn't reply, rushing like an avalanche was about to swallow him, trying to catch up with Caleb, who'd covered a fair piece of ground. Pushing between branches, he practically stumbled into the supplies sled, stopped right there. Caleb and the men had disengaged from pushing it and faced each other in an attitude of having arrived.

Breathing hard, Eriks took in the scene, crestfallen to see just more trees and snow, no blackened kettle of simmering soup hanging from a tripod over a crackling fire, no cabin, no tent, nothing.

"Farmer Barons let us stay at the dairy in exchange for running supplies out here," Caleb was saying to the men, sounding defensive. "That was our deal."

"Yah," chirped Kristaps, standing behind Caleb at shoulder height.

"But if there's no more supplies coming, then we won't be needing you to run them. You see?" Wagtail countered, the shape of his white cape indicating arms akimbo.

"But here we are," Caleb said. "Because we did run the supplies, including guns." He expelled a weary breath. "So didn't we earn a place to stay?"

"Look, no one wants to break faith with you, Caleb," Wagtail said. "You did your part. You hold up your end every time. Now have the good sense to get away. Frankly, we can't spare a man to defend you. We can't feed one, two, three hungry pups." He pointed to Kristaps and Eriks as he counted.

"I'm eighteen," Eriks said.

"And you eat like Lāčplēsis," said Wagtail. "Don't feed strays, Haralds," he scolded, as if he had eyes in the back of his head and knew Haralds was about to hand out spuds. "Don't encourage them. Not when I got men eating snow."

Haralds slumped. "For your own good," he muttered, tightening a burlap drawstring. He lit a cigarette and the flame illumed under the brim of his homburg, for a second showing the affable liveliness that had etched Haralds's thin face. He pointed into the dark, saying, "I know an outfit to the East has women and children."

"I want to talk to the Architect about this," Caleb persisted. "I think he'd give me a chance."

"Nay. There's no need to bother him about something so straightforward," Wagtail said. "Tell you what though. Looks like between the three of you, you got two pairs of boots and one pickax. I'll give one or two of you a job. *Temporarily.* For as long as it takes you to turn a hole into an underground bunker."

"Ground's frozen solid," Caleb said.

"Didn't say it would be an easy job. And furthermore I'll fire a laggard in a drop-dead minute. That's the best I can offer you scamps. So get some shut-eye. You can stay 'til morning. Then cast lots or in some manner decide who stays and who goes."

"We'll be faster as a tunneling team of three," Eriks said. "What if we're an all or nothing deal?"

"Then I pick nothing," Wagtail retorted. "But I'm keeping that pickax either way." He exhaled, tugging his mattress pad-cape. "Look, I wish we were in a position to help you rascals. I'm sorry you were kicked from the nest. But each orphan I adopt worsens the odds for my men by that much. And likely gets you killed. That's what we're talking about here."

Wagtail grabbed the bundled hay from the sledge and heaved it to the ground. With a nod to Haralds, they began sliding away with the groceries.

"See you in church," Wagtail said.

Eriks watched them move off, his last hope crumbling like a frostbitten toe.

"Yah. Goodnight, Captain," Caleb said, quietly.

Captain? Eriks was doubly aggrieved to learn he'd not only been rejected, but by someone of stature. "Keep them dry, Aivars," Captain Wagtail said over his shoulder. He meant the guns.

Aivars carried the rifles to the backside of a snow berm. His cap-badge trophies glinted as his head turned, scanning the environs. He bent down to unstrap his snowshoes, and didn't reappear. Kristaps and Caleb followed, dragging the hay between them. Yet when Eriks clomped to the other side of the berm no one was there. At his knees a flap of oilcloth was lifted at the corner, revealing a black hole the size of a window on a bus.

Eriks unbuckled his snowshoes and, as he squatted down to peer inside, lost his balance and slipped, sliding through the berm and down a few meters into a dark, frozen den, not stopping until he bumped into Kristaps. Sitting on his tailbone, Eriks raised his arms and touched the ceiling of the ice cave, but was otherwise unable to judge its dimensions.

Moonlight seeped through the opening and Eriks's eyes adjusted. Aivars was crouched and tugging something heavy, finally dislodging a plank. "It's not your mother's, but it's dry," he said, referring to a sarcophagus-sized hole in the frozen floor.

"Cozy," Caleb said, stepping down in the hole and helping Aivars remove another board.

Aivars handed Caleb the inferior rifles they'd brought. As Caleb laid them into some rustling material, he said, "Kristaps, prop up your snowshoes and hang your rags. They'll be freeze dried by sunrise."

Kristaps started pulling off his outer layers.

Eriks fetched his snowshoes and did the same. Shivering in his long johns, he groped his way to the sharply hewn edge of the pit before removing his soaked shoes and socks. The snowgrave-gunlocker seemed to be paneled with split pine. He stepped down into it, relieved that his numb feet landed on a thick pad of dry moss, and sat down carefully. Aivars tossed in the hay. Eriks spread it around, stretching his legs and sinking into the crackle and scratch of dry grasses and bark.

Kristaps dropped in, taking the slim spot in the middle. He grabbed an armful of leaves and straw and pulled it over him, burying his feet and legs.

"Good night, young princes," Aivars said, wrangling a plank back into position across the opening.

Eriks flattened down. There was not enough room to sit up with the covering in place.

"Sweet dreams of Russian heads on pikes," Aivars said, dropping the final board, the lid on the casket.

The darkness was arresting. Eriks lay, hands folded over chest, eyes open and seeing nothing. He expelled the breath he'd been holding. Brain empty as a black slate, whoever he'd thought he'd been, erased. Even the sting of Stalin's whip was a blurred memory from the distant land of the living. The unlikely moment with Zelma, remote as a whiff of lilac in a gale force storm. The algebraic problem involving three guys, two pairs of boots and one pickax, an abstraction with solution contained in the null set. He lay in the earth and was powerless to change anything above ground. In fact, he might as well stay here and die. Ice water splat on his face. He said, "Don't bother taking me out of this hole."

"You get really bleak when you're hungry," Caleb said with a yawn. "Your stomach will adjust, mate."

"Just shut up," Eriks wanted to say, imagining the aroma of roasted potato.

Kristaps kept bumping him.

Eriks was about to snarl at the kid to keep his hands to himself, when he rolled over to find Kristaps holding out a roasted potato in one hand, and in the other an egg!

"Kristaps, you're saving my life!" Eriks cried, wanting to leap over the moon. But there wasn't even room to sit up, so he turned on his side, head on elbow, holding the bounty with unspeakable gratitude. "While we were dragging your skinny butt through the forest you were rifling the goods?"

"You can't rely on the hospitality of partisans," Kristaps said, rustling in the grass.

"Thank you," Caleb said.

"Yah, *paldies*," Eriks said, excited but deciding to eat slowly this time. "And forgive me for ever being uppity about your tendency to steal things."

"*Loudzu*," Kristaps said. "It is Christmas Eve, after all."

That sucked the chatter out of the crypt.

Christmas Eve tugged powerful heartstrings, magnified by heritage-soaked rum-and-raisin memories of every Christmas Eve before it. Family gathered in the penthouse above the spellbinding view of the lit up park and the Opera House. The smell of his father's pipe, gingerbread, and wax while Eriks lit the candles on the tree. Last year, as Eriks had recited a *daina* to get a present, no one could have foreseen that by the following Christmas his parents would be arrested, and Eriks would be essentially buried alive, his sole gift a potato, given by shoeless Kristaps.

"There's a Hannukah saying going 'round the ghetto this year," Caleb said, cracking an eggshell. "*Where they want to bury us alive, we pull the gravediggers in with us.* Sounds catchier in Polish."

"Sweet," Kristaps said.

As Eriks nibbled, an angel's breath of music floated to his ear. "Is that a flute?" he asked, wondering if he was hallucinating.

"That's Aivars," Caleb said.

"Aivars plays the flute?" Eriks asked, unable to imagine that the man who'd terrified him with rifle blasts also produced these delicate reedy notes.

"Yah, made from the bone of a Chekist," Kristaps said. "He draws the enemy out with a tune, then he sends them to the Shade Mother."

"He's pulling your leg," Caleb said, chuckling. "Funny, though, how he blathers about that ancient lore like its real."

"He's crazy enough to do it," Kristaps said.

"He's the deadest shot in these parts, that's the truth," Caleb said. "Kristaps! Why's the dugout smell like dog farts?"

With a moan, Caleb writhed upward, widening the crack between boards and nosing for fresh air that fell inside heavily and cold.

Kristaps was squirming and hooting about stink bombs, acting childish.

Annoyed, Eriks then remembered how young the kid was. Caleb looked out for him like a big brother. Eyes moist with holiday goodwill, Eriks said, "I will strike out for that other outfit. You two are a team. You should stay together." He didn't feel as brave as he thought he sounded.

"Just hold on. You don't know the ropes yet," Caleb said. "You could get lost or stumble into a hot spot."

"Let's make our own hole and hibernate 'til spring," Kristaps said.

"This hole was made last summer," Caleb said. "When the ground was soft and a few paranoid folks, who were absolutely right, started stashing weapons. Now that it's the dead of winter, we'd have to blast and burn and thaw and hack every centimeter to dig something this grand."

"Well, then what?" Eriks asked, dispirited that even this miserable pit was beyond his grasp.

"I do not know," Caleb said, yawning again. "I just rise in the morning and figure it out fresh every day. Been lucky like that for over a year now."

"Hmmph." Eriks said, rolling over and, in so doing, forcing the other two to also shift positions. "I know a thing or two about luck," he said, "and this is not it. I may never be warm again. My face aches and a thousand burning needles are pricking my thawing feet. Nay. *Lucky* was me yesterday with Zelma."

Suddenly Eriks realized in a rush that he hadn't even asked Zelma how her errand had gone, the trip she'd dreaded making into the treacherous, Cheka-infested, one-lane village. *Fuck!* He was dense, as well as unlucky. What did it matter anyway, he conceded, sinking heavier into the earth. Nothing did anymore. His chest hurt, lungs in irons, every breath a dull stab of pain. Patikamspils. That was the place.

K. Smiltens, 1943.

- 11 -

ERIKS COULDN'T SEE THE VILE CREATURE. *He felt its sharp-clawed, gluttonous presence, leering into the tomb.*

"Who are you?" it asked in a rumbling, disembodied voice.

"I was nursed by all Latvian mothers," Eriks said, and was frightened by his own utterance, which sounded like a congregation of flat voices reading in unison. "My soul is the souls of all Latvians lying under the soil of the Motherland."

"There's no such place... your Motherland." The evil thing shifted shape. Entering a suit of armor it became a knight. A wave of terror rippled across the land.

"You are Loudmouth. Glamour Boy. Pup!" mocked the knight from behind a beveled face grate. "Your so-called nation has no history, just old wives' tales, folk songs, proverbs, incanted by farmers and midwives. Hearsay!"

A muzzled dog was whining. Humming filled Eriks's ears, getting louder, buzzing like a sawmill in his head. The knight's laughter grew loud and diabolical, until the visor snapped open. Eriks saw a heart-shaped face in the helmet. A million lit candles on Christmas trees flared and were snuffed. Silence. Eriks was floating, looking down at his corpse in its earth coffin, wreathed with frost flowers and ice ribbons.

He woke with a jerk, sweating. Thank God, he thought with a gasp, it's all a nightmare. Eyes opened, still dark. Hands ran over the chilblains on his arms. He couldn't move, trapped between a slab of frozen pine and shivering Kristaps. His heart caved. This was his reality. He would die if he didn't change it.

The fibers of a plan wove together all at once in bold geometry. Muscles insisted he rise. He pushed the planks off like a pavement-cracking weed.

The hour was late morning, judging by the height of the sun bursting through holes in the clouds and making odd patches of snow glisten. A few snowflakes were falling. The world was a white canvas on which anything might be painted.

Eriks strode toward where he heard the volley of men's voices, and soon saw the outlaws at a small fire. Nearby, a thin plume of steam rose from the top of a *pirts*. The sauna looked smartly constructed of birch trunks, uniformly as thick as Eriks's forearm, leaning together teepee-style.

Eriks walked up as Haralds was saying, "The priority is to get some powder or make it." He lowered the brim of his homburg and tugged his black frock coat around his thin frame. "Otherwise we can do nothing."

"One thing we cannot do is nothing," Captain Wagtail said, startling Eriks who had not noticed the portly man, a credit to the mattress pad camouflage. "We either grow or we perish."

"We can keep on wire-cutting," said a new face. "Pull up rail ties."

There were several men standing around whom Eriks had not seen before. But his attention snapped to a man sitting on a tree stump, wearing boots and a towel, naked from the waist up except for a black beret. The man's skin looked flushed, like he'd just stepped out of the pirts and was steamed to the bone. He held a besom, still wet from dripping water on the hot rocks, and swatted his back with the whisk of dried birch leaves, emitting a waft of wintergreen. Executive decisions were often made in the serenity of the pirts, Eriks knew, and he bet this man was the Architect, whom Captain Wagtail had referred to the night before. This was the man Eriks must persuade.

"Just be sure we don't cut communication wires the Germans will need when they come to liberate us," Haralds said.

"I hate Nazis," Captain Wagtail said, lifting a small branch and tossing it on the fire, "but anyone opposing Stalin has got to be considered an ally." As Eriks came up to the fire ring, Wagtail said, "*Labrite, Glamour Boy.*"

"Good Morning," Eriks replied, aware that all eyes were on him and his posh overcoat. The plan that was brilliant a moment ago now seemed idiotic. He looked at the faces in the loosely formed ring, seeing in the men's features some hardness that he'd been sheltered from until three days ago. He ran his hands over wild hair that would never lie down.

"So, you're Gailis, like the department store?" said the Architect.

"Yah," Eriks said, a lump in his throat. The moment for his proposal was now. He took a breath and straightened up, noticing as he did that he was taller than everyone present. "I—me and my friends—we could be an asset to you, if you'd have us." Faltering and feeling a fool, he spoke faster, to pitch his idea before anyone cut him off. "Granted, I don't have a gun to defend myself with at the moment, but I'm not coming here with my hand out. I have intelligence and a plan, a plan that could yield a trove of weapons."

Eriks cleared his throat and continued, "But it'll take serious nerve to pull it off. So, if you can't stomach it, I'll look for backup from that outfit with the women and children."

The men laughed at that, to Eriks's surprise.

"Let's hear it," said the Architect.

Eriks threw out his chest and described his "live bait" scheme, a plan drawing from everything he'd seen recently.

The Architect leaned back, listening, saying nothing.

Captain Wagtail interrupted frequently, pounding Eriks with questions.

Determined to prove that he was worth feeding and sheltering, Eriks embellished the upside potential of his plan, getting modern weaponry, and downplayed the likelihood it was a deadly boondoggle. He elaborated in a detached manner, almost forgetting that it would be his flesh used to draw out the Cheka, until he saw the white faces of Caleb and Kristaps who had come to the fire ring and stood listening to the roles Eriks had in mind for them.

"The ambush has to take place in that particular village," Eriks explained, "because the sole NKVD outpost is located two kilometers away down an isolated road, which is also the only point of access." He was betting the farm on Zelma's pillow talk. "The authorities there are known to be among the most strict and zealous of the NKVD."

"That's a fact you can take to the bank," said a snaggle-toothed man, nodding.

"I like it, Glamour Boy," said Aivars. "I say we move on it straight away."

Great, Eriks thought, nodding to Aivars. He had the insane killer's vote. The plan must be madness.

"Mayhem. Could be absolute mayhem," Captain Wagtail said. "I'd want to see this road. Surveil the village and assess the habits of the local Cheka thoroughly before committing the men."

"It's not right," said a man wearing a hunter's vest. "It's not a boy's place to hazard such a risk on behalf of grown men."

"A youngster has a better chance of getting away with it," said another.

"You have to give us a chance to prove ourselves," Eriks said. "Because if we can't find a place with you, then I don't know where we go next." He felt his eyes tingle at his pitiable situation. "Maybe Kristaps won't have to be involved."

"We'll discuss it," said the Architect. "Why don't you boys warm up in the pirts. Get a bite to eat."

Eriks was heartened that, if nothing else, his bid had earned him another morsel. He stripped his clothes and ducked through the entrance into the dry heat of the pirts, inhaling the comforting aromas of birch and tar. Warmth at last stilled his shivering core and he imagined telling Zelma about how he'd led an ambush. He pictured her admiring him holding the trophy he'd win from this gambit, his own gun.

That very morning, the Architect, Aivars and Captain Wagtail set out to verify Eriks's claims. Three days later, they had not returned. Eriks worried that the scouts would tromp into camp and say, "You and your bogus idea can hit the road." He dreaded that they would come back to say, "You're brilliant. The plan is a go." Then there was always the chance they'd never be seen again. The prickly wait was only bearable because the boys were allowed to use the pirts and sleep in the gun cache. Kristaps spent happy hours feeding slim rations of hay to the band's perky, but ribby horse. They dined with the renegades on reindeer sausage, pine nuts and birch tea, as well as the foodstuffs from the dairy, watching the stores deplete rapidly.

Eriks used the time to drill, exchanging fake punches with Caleb and Kristaps, as they'd done in the barn.

"It's got to look real," he said, swaying and holding fists in front of his face. "We got to be bodacious. Fizzing!" He ripped at Caleb with a jab-cross combo and a peppering of rabbit punches. "What we want is for some spineless jerk to report us to the Cheka. Woe-hoe!"

Caleb countered with an upper cut that would've clocked Eriks good, had it connected.

Eriks nearly slipped on ice, but regained his balance, bracing a hand against a tree bough. "We have to pose an epic threat," he said, "so every Chekist in the vicinity wants to arrest us. We need to be... disturbing."

"That's crazy!" Kristaps cried, perching on a fallen tree trunk. "We're gonna try to get caught by the Cheka? They'll fry our giblets!"

Eriks snapped his fingers. "We'll dress as mummers."

"Mummers, what?" Caleb said. "Translation, please."

Kristaps brightened instantly. "My father sang in a Budēļi group. He was a stork."

"I thought we needed to look dangerous," Caleb said. "Not like caroling wildlife."

"There's something kāpost galva unnerving about mummering," Eriks said. "Come on." He beckoned to Kristaps. "We got to find materials for making masks, and anything freakish or bizarre."

"Ask that hunter," Caleb said, "the one who makes the tasty sausage."

The hunter gave the boys a matted old black bear pelt, for what he called welcome distraction. Draping it over Eriks's head, the man fashioned laces to hold the pelt in place. He lifted tufts of fur and shaped round little ears with a razor.

Kristaps watched in fascination as Eriks blackened his eyes with charred cork. He screamed with merriment as Eriks lumbered after him Frankenstein-style, with rigid outstretched arms.

"So, this mumming," Caleb said, breaking off branches, trying to find a pair that looked like antlers. "It's a Latvian winter ritual?"

"Not what my family does," Eriks said. "I never have mummered personally. It's old, old, old-timey stuff. Folks still do it for frolic, though, as a way to visit neighbors. Not that it'll really change the next year's fortunes. But there's something mystical at the deep bottom of it, some power I can't explain. The Communists won't abide it."

Caleb held his "antlers" to the sides of his head and bellowed a buck mating call.

Kristaps copied him.

"Now, how to make them stay put," Caleb said, as the branches fell from the fold in his hat.

"Hold on," Eriks said, remembering something he'd seen in the gun cache. In minutes he was in the ice cave, under the planks, searching through the dried grass. He found the solution in the stash of obsolete armaments. It was perfect.

"Here," he told Caleb. "Try on this gas mask."

"Hot damn!" Caleb said, holding up the contraption for a look. "That's some legitimate prankster garb."

"From the Great War," Eriks said, helping Caleb don the oiled canvas mask, which completely covered his head, rendering him faceless.

Leather circles holding glass lenses gave Caleb the eyes of a giant insect. A metal filter canister hung around his chin like an alien proboscis.

"Tuck your antlers under the straps, like that," Eriks said, and stepped back to study the effect.

Caleb secured his antler branches and topped the whole affair with a fur cap, becoming a netherworld stag.

Kristaps whistled. "That'll put the frightens on them."

"Puts the frightens on me," Eriks said, unsettled where he was leading his friends.

"Just buck up!" Caleb said, his voice loud and muffled.

"Ha!" cried Kristaps, alerting Eriks to the pun.

"I can't," Eriks retorted, modeling the pelt. "I'm bearly dressed."

"Caleb's going stag," Kristaps shot in.

"Yah, well, you shouldn't run with his elk," Eriks said.

"That's not what I herd," Caleb said.

Eriks was racking his brain for an antler pun, when he heard a low whistle and spun around to see that Aivars had stealthed up.

"Straight outta the Shade realm," Aivars said, approving the masquerade.

Captain Wagtail was walking over, too.

Eriks suddenly felt like an ass in the mumming get-up, but Wagtail didn't mention it.

The captain planted his legs and folded his arms under his cape before pronouncing, "Your plan is not impossible."

The bottom dropped out of Eriks's stomach.

"Utterly reckless, but it's the best we got at the moment," Wagtail said. "If you still want to do it, we're leaving tonight."

K. Smiltens, 1946.

-12-

IGOR VOLKOV SAT WHERE JANIS Pērkons used to sit, ensconced in a deep executive armchair. From the loft office, he overlooked the factory floor of what used to be Pērkons Leather Works. His feet rested on the desk, which was topped in supple, rich leather that made his boots look cheap as tarpaper. Life was unfair, Igor brooded, lamenting his mistake. He should have forced Pērkons to fabricate the superior custom boots *before* reporting the capitalist as a Harmful Element. The NKVD had reacted unpredictably swiftly in banishing Pērkons and his employees. Then a swarm of state shit-heads had pranced in, not respecting that it was Igor who was to credit for confiscating the Leather Works, Igor who should be in charge.

He missed Pērkons. Besides having a bigshot wardrobe, Pērkons showed respect, paying tribute, cash and a 22-carat cigarette case, in exchange for Igor's blind eye. But Igor had taken the bribe and snitched on

Pērkons anyway, because he despised the wealthy man. Igor had erred, he concluded, appreciating the weight of the gold case in his pocket. He should have milked Pērkons dry, amassing a small, secret fortune... in case life became drastic.

Learn from the cat, Igor told himself. The cat toys with the mouse at leisure. Igor could have dawdled long enough to make the old craftsman eat belt stew, and other pleasurable deeds. He could have raided Pērkons's closet and by wearing his shirts be seen as a powerful person to respect. There would still have been plenty of time to later gain points with the secret police.

Dealing with the NKVD had been a vile and wicked experience. The agents put Igor to grunt work. To make matters worse they installed a foreman who, to Volkov's disgust, was an Asian breed, an ugly, pig-nosed Buryat low-life scum from some backwater near Mongolia. His workers were rowdy low-class menials. Igor Volkov was descended from Cossacks. Taking orders from an oversized, slant-eyed nomad sucked all pride from him.

"*Komsomal!*" The foreman didn't deign to learn Igor's name, stupidly shouting the Communist youth union as if summoning a boy scout. "Get moving before I put a boot up your ass." The workers were manhandling the industrial-sized immersion drums through the rolling loading doors, snorting and swearing.

Volkov panicked at the fervent scramble to disassemble capital equipment and ship it to Russia. Such work was beneath him. It was cowardly and disgraceful to act afraid that Germans would chase Russians out of Latvia.

Tools were dumped into barrels and rolled away clanking. Someone cursed at finding that the heavy cutting table, with its massive iron underside, was bolted to the cement floor.

An intellectual destined for greatness, Igor could not degrade himself to common toil. He exalted labor as much as the next Communist. And when a job fit his extraordinary, magnificent person he would be the zenith of discipline, and would rise above all other men.

But the present dire situation was a horrific humiliation. Inside this factory inferiors from the hinterland treated him like a mule. Out on the street, beautiful blond Latvian females reviled him. And a photograph of the family Pērkons propped on the desk, mocked and tormented him. Igor had never been immortalized by a camera. Yet he'd seen this inferior insect Kārlis Pērkons, the same age as Igor, who was born into wealth and never had to fight for his rightful place in a brutal world, memorialized for posterity in at least two photographs. Igor imagined tracking down Kārlis Pērkons and executing him. One day he would be powerful enough to punish everyone who looked down on him, everyone he hated.

The wooden stairway shuddered as somebody ascended to the loft.

Igor felt giddy about the inevitable confrontation with the foreman.

The door opened without a knock. Igor kept staring at his boots, channeling rage into the look of his eye. The look alone was often enough to make these weaklings back away.

"Igor Volkov." A smart Russian accent, the speaker had authority.

Igor's head snapped up.

A uniformed soldier sneered down his nose at him. "Papers."

Igor swung his legs off the desk and stood. The soldier's haughty mien was insulting, but Igor overlooked that and hurried to show his Komsomal

Communist Youth Union card, eager to know if the time had finally come.

"Sign here," said the soldier, holding out a clipboard with a list of gathered signatures.

Igor signed, forcing his hand not to shake.

The soldier handed over an officious envelope and departed.

Igor had been expecting this since he turned nineteen. He slit the envelope with Pērkons's letter opener and removed an ordinary, non-letterhead paper. The missive had fill-in-the-blank lines completed with longhand Cyrillic script.

Evidence of call to fulfill military obligation No. 1272.

Name: Igor Volkov

Igor silently cursed his lack of an important sounding middle name. He should change his name, as had dear Comrade Stalin.

Date of birth: November 13, 1922

Seeing his birth date in print bolstered Igor's sense of destiny, as he was born the same year as the Soviet Union.

Rank or status of society: petty bourgeois

He bristled. That would change. This call-up notice was a step toward power, which would lead to wealth, and the women would follow.

The letter stated Igor was obligated to appear at a nearby recruitment office. Draftees were given THREE DAYS to take care of household affairs before reporting for service. Orders and consequences for not obeying were explicit. The missive bore the red authenticity stamp of the USSR. Igor felt the thrill of being swept up in the hurricane of worldwide Communism.

The door slammed open, and in sauntered the hulking foreman. "I will have you arrested for slacking," he threatened.

"I have higher orders." Igor waved the conscription

notice, guessing the foreman didn't even know how to read.

But the brute's ugly features registered comprehension right away, folding arms and blocking the door. "The Army can survive without your lazy ass until you load this factory to the rails."

Heart trilling, Igor sidestepped the desk and pushed past the foreman, whose jaw dropped. "Mine is the holy duty of all able bodied male Soviets, to serve the 11th Red Army, Baltic Military Operation," he proclaimed. Igor feared the henchmen in the workshop would try to apprehend him, but they were straining to cart off the tool bench.

"Load it yourself, Comrade."

K. Smiltens, 1949.

-13-

THE HIKE TO PATIKAMSPILS DRUBBED the jitters out of Eriks. It entailed a midnight trek back toward the dairy, and then a lengthy march beyond, this time accompanied by a phalanx of fifteen men. Eriks was buoyed by the camaraderie. There was the Architect and his two educated sons, Captain Wagtail, who'd served in the military, and Homburg Haralds. There was Snaggle-Wit who vowed to hide his two drafted sons in the woods rather than sacrifice them for the benefit of Russia, an enterprising sailor and his nephew referred to as the Hawks of Pavilosta, and a brawny fellow called Stone Hill, on account of his stubborn streak. Nicknaming abounded to avoid Chekist retribution against families. Nobody could endure the savage backlash like the one dealt to the family of Aivars the Lonely, whom Eriks secretly thought should be called Mad Aivars. Bee-in-your-Cap Kristaps travelled with the Hunter on horseback. True to their moniker, there was no chit-chat when Silent Forest was on the move.

In the dark and quietude, Eriks turned over every detail he could remember Zelma saying about the village... *the most rabid militia you never want to meet... lounging around NKVD command post, waiting for someone to punish... villagers would report their own mothers to get in good with the Ivans.*

"We're not far now," Wagtail finally said, with a nod toward the sunrise. "We stop here and eat."

The last of the food had been saved for this breakfast. Eriks took the slice of black bread as turn-back-now proof that this wanna-be partisan band was hopelessly under-fueled against Stalin. He searched his universe for a source of strength besides food, some font that couldn't be arrested, tortured, deported or collectivized. Revenge didn't inspire him. He wasn't fighting for revenge. He had no choice but the course ahead. He chewed the bread, fortified by knowing the rye had been grown on this land, his country. He felt like praying. All around were trees. The trees. He awakened to their energy, even as it coursed in the dried veins of his hiking staff.

Eriks put on the bear pelt with intention suiting a ritual, not speaking as Caleb applied the eyeblack and it dribbled from the corners of his eyes. The disguise gave him a buffer of anonymity, as if it was not *he* risking his life. And the beast personna linked him with some ancient force, the one he sensed lying dormant in the tangled roots beneath the frozen ground. After all, four Baltic tribes had struggled for their territories in these woods, appealing to local spirits, tree or animal, for strength. Why shouldn't he? Not understanding the connection, Eriks quietly snapped off the end of a fir branch, and poked it through his lapel buttonhole.

Captain Wagtail was coming over, and Eriks

wondered briefly if the captain felt similarly empowered by his white, mattress pad cape. Aivars, in the white camos, was with him, both hands ready on his rifle. The Architect followed, looking professional in a crisp white shirt over thermals and sharply trimmed beard and moustache.

"Let's be sure we're on the same page," the Architect said. He held out a strip of birch bark marked by confident pencil strokes. "Here's our village. The traditional layout, shops and a tavern around the town square. There's only one passable road into town, with high frozen berms on either side of it. About two kilometers down the road from the village is this old manor house." He tapped its symbol on the bark. "Command center for the local militia and NKVD. They're fully staffed and well-armed. Takes them from five to twenty minutes to ride into town depending on their level of enthusiasm."

Eriks understood the situation, theoretically.

"Keep the sun at your left shoulder and you'll reach the village square in about half an hour," Wagtail said. "Meanwhile, we'll fan out and take positions farther up along the road."

"We're all in, Glamour Boy," Aivars said. Under the camouflaged hood, the cap badge trophies on his beret lined up precisely straight. "Go out there and throw a seven."

Climbing over the tall, icy berm in snowshoes was a clumsy affair landing Eriks on his buttocks. He scrambled to his feet brushing snow off his pelt, hoping none of the men were watching. The road was empty in both directions, a snowy lane glittering like sugar in the late morning sun.

Caleb removed his glasses, upended a bottle of whiskey to his mouth, swished and spit it out, spraying his clothes. He pulled on his gas mask, and adjusted his antlers and fur hat. Eriks, likewise, doused himself with the booze perfume and handed the bottle back. Caleb exhaled a wavering stream of white vapor. He tapped the whiskey bottle with a spoon, a slow beat. Eriks calmed down, matching his breathing to the steady rhythm of the bottle-drum.

"Here we go, mate," Caleb said, pivoting toward the village. He started down the road with heavy steps, drumming evenly, the gait of a person heading where he never wanted to arrive... pretending to be drunk and wearing the eerie stag getup with the same aplomb that he approached every daunting task.

Eriks was damned grateful for meeting Caleb on the train. Now he had a brother to walk with down the road.

"There's special songs, right?" Caleb asked, his voice muffled by the mask.

"Yah," Eriks said, searching his mind, which was not in song mode. *"Nu, tetin, ziemas svetki. Father it's the winter festival."* He couldn't remember more.

"And I've frozen a testicle," Caleb supplied. "Is there anything edible?"

Father it's the winter festival." Eriks sang.

"I call it the *whimper* festival," Caleb said, hee-hawing Eriks's every verse.

The road had been recently cleared, and it wasn't long before Eriks saw where it ended at a cluster of two-storied, half-timbered buildings. The song left his head, as he walked into the village square. Lesser roads radiated from there, more like footpaths used by townsfolk going about their business under shrouded, hunched shoulders. He and Caleb gravitated toward a dais in the center of the plaza, where uprooted cement and twisted iron jutted up, as if a statue of the village hero once honored there had been toppled. Shop windows edging the square were shuttered tight. No sign indicated which door lead to the public house, but Eriks deduced its location by following the most trafficked path, cobblestones showing through the slushy snow, to where assorted snowshoes leaned against the wall. He and Caleb unlaced and added theirs to the collection.

Entering the tavern, Eriks had to duck so his bear head cleared the lintel. While his eyes adjusted to the dim light, he took stock of the premises. A couple dozen locals appeared to be grabbing an early lunch, a joyless bunch, probably washing down bread and herring with a beer before returning to work. He filled his chest with a deep breath and sallied forth.

"Children, let's go mummering, on a winter's eve," Eriks sang, plodding toward the bar. Caleb followed, *tinking* double-time on the bottle.

"We bring blessings of fertility to this canteen," Eriks called out as he passed a crowded table. "Heavy crops! And babies! Be blessed with many *Latvian* babies." He sensed a communal intake of breath at that, and covered the awkward silence with a belch, as someone muttered, "troublemakers".

"We also frighten away evil spirits," he said, sliding onto a bar stool, "and you know who I mean."

The bartender's expression was hidden behind a plush, white caricature moustache that curled up at the ends. He faced Eriks stiffly, acting like he hadn't heard the remark.

"You're supposed to welcome us with a treat," Eriks told him. "Two Balsams will do."

"You have money?" the bartender demanded.

"My friend's buying," Eriks said. "He's a deer. Bah! My funds have been frozen."

Seeing Caleb pull out rubles, the bartender took down the brown crockery flagon labeled *Rigas Black Balsams* and poured some into two shot glasses. While he diluted each with vodka, Eriks read the ornate black and gold label.

"Distilled uniquely in Riga," Eriks remarked. "An ancient mixture of forest herbs with mysterious properties. Heard this all my life," Eriks said, sliding a glass to Caleb. "You'd think, by now, the mysteries would be solved." He lifted his glass to the portrait behind the bar. "Here's to General Stalin," Eriks said. "Although..." He opened his gullet and threw back the shot, "I like it better when he wears the pink dress."

The elixir burned going down, steadying Eriks with a worldly hand. He felt his heart beating in his neck, his precious heartbeat, and was not bothered by the bartender fussing, "I'll have none of that. And I mean Get Out. You with the horns, you too! Out!"

"All right, we'll skedaddle," Eriks said, scooting his stool from the bar. "How 'bout one quick skit first, though, for the sake of tradition." Turning to face the most populous table in the pub, he said, "Heard the one about *The Knock at Night*?"

A graybeard shifted in his seat, unable to take his eyes off faceless Caleb, who swayed behind Eriks's elbow.

Eriks put on his campiest melodrama. "One night there was a loud knock at the door of a certain house."

He acted it out, pounding on the table, rattling lunch plates.

"Watch it!" roared a man in an argyle vest.

"The family inside was too afraid to answer it. So they cowered in their bedrooms." Eriks hid behind trembling forearms. "But the knocking got louder and LOUDER." Eriks moved down the table, darting between the patrons and hammering the table with his fists.

"*Kāpost galva* fool!" cursed a man with a mouthful. Eriks snagged a fried potato off the plate of a man picking his teeth, and ate it, while a fellow lighting a cigarette looked on with wooden disapproval. A man in green suspenders scraped his chair across the floor and strode to the coat rack. Eriks stared, barely able to keep talking as the man left the tavern with a slam of the door. Was that the wished-for informant? If so, how long before the Cheka came? Five minutes, twenty?

Caleb kicked him.

"Anyway," Eriks resumed, "the family pretended to be asleep, 'til finally the bastards start breaking down the door!"

The bartender was coming around the bar to get him, so Eriks puffed his chest and spoke faster.

"Inside the house, the grandfather thinks to himself, 'I'm an old man. I'm going to die soon anyway. I'll go see what they want.' So he gets out of bed and goes to the door. A minute later he rushes back shouting for joy, 'Good news, loved ones. *The building's on fire!*'"

"Ha ha!" Eriks held his belly, snorting. "Get it?"

"You're outta here," the bartender said, grasping Eriks under the arms. "Time for some fresh air."

"Oh! Be a doll and put up a couple mummers for the night," Eriks said.

But the bartender pushed Eriks toward the door,

hissing in his ear, "You'll be killed, you idiot. The militia here is severe. Go home. For godsakes, go sober up."

Eriks, a head taller than the barkeep, allowed himself to be manhandled, until he passed another full table. Then he applied his feet like brakes and leaned into a sallow-faced guy, saying, "You know why the Cheka works in groups of three? One can read, one can write, and the third man keeps an eye on the two intellectuals! Ha ha ha. Buy me a drink." He grabbed the man by the collar.

The sallow man got up with surprising speed and took a swing, which Eriks barely dodged, breaking loose of the bartender.

"Comrade, if I hit you, you'll need a travel pass," Eriks said, waving his fist, everything alive and all juices flowing. He glimpsed another man get up to leave, this one in a double-breasted jacket. Then clenched knuckles hit his eye and he staggered back, crashing into chairs. He tried to regain his footing and strike back, but his arms were pinned. Caleb's buck mating call brayed over the fracas. People shoved and dragged Eriks toward the door, a zoetrope of scuffing arms and legs seen through the throbbing slit of an eye. Bright cold air hit him before he slammed into frozen cobblestones. The heels of his hands broke his skid, stinging. He righted himself, looking up in time to see Caleb ejected from the tavern, legs pedaling for balance, gas mask maligned and antlers askew.

Eriks grabbed a handful of snow and held it to his tender, taut eye socket. His head was thumping and the job was not done.

His ears pricked up at the rhythm of soft thuds coming down the road. He looked up quick, relieved and disappointed to see it was not the Cheka coming, but the flopping footfalls of Kristaps's cardboard shoes. His muffler and pointy knit cap, bobbing as he ran, caught the attention of the handful of villagers in the square.

"Well, the squirt's right on cue," Eriks said.

"He shouldn't even be here," Caleb mumbled.

Eriks strode to the center of the square, cutting through a young family, to block Kristaps's path. "Not so fast, little comrade," he said, snatching the boy's cap. He waved the cap high and low, out of Kristaps's reach.

"Gimme back my hat," Kristaps said, his voice shrill.

Eriks clutched Kristaps by the lapels and whispered, "What's going on?"

"Nothing. The Hunter's over there, behind some trees."

Eriks looked down the road. It was peaceful as a Christmas card. His plan was losing momentum. Gutted, he pushed the kid away.

"Can't quit now," Caleb said, grabbing Kristaps's arms from behind.

"Leave me alone," Kristaps cried.

"Why aren't you in school, boy, learning Russian," Eriks bullied, rearing a fist.

"Help," Kristaps yelled. "Somebody help me!"

Eriks backhanded Kristaps's round cheek.

"Cowardly brute," said an old woman walking across the square.

Eriks turned to her. "I love what you've done with your hair," he yelled, scooping a handful of snow. "How did you get it to come out of one nostril like that?" He threw a loosely packed snowball, hitting the old lady on the shoulder. Then he punched Kristaps in the gut. Kristaps timed his gasping, double-over like a pro. The attack looked real.

Eriks glanced up expectantly, and looked around. No one was watching the performance! The windows of the pub were shuttered tight. No one was coming to help Kristaps. "Will no one stick his neck out to save a kid anymore?" he muttered, swinging Kristaps by the collar. "What does it take to draw out the police in this village?"

"Destruction," Caleb said, picking up a hunk of cement from the dais and hefting it from hand to gloved hand. He took aim at a second-story picture window on the corner building and heaved it. The glass shattered in a chiming cascade to the walkway below, where a young woman scurried away with a tiny shriek. The old lady and every passerby fled the square.

Eriks turned to watch the road, expecting the militia to descend in a fury.

Kristaps was looking in the opposite direction when his face drained of all color.

A leggy black horse was stepping down one of the footpaths between the buildings, an NKVD agent in the saddle. His red hammer-and-sickle cap badge glinted in the noon sun as he looked down at the broken glass and up at Caleb, and reined his mount into the square.

Eriks's stomach flooded with acid. He'd expected the Cheka to charge from the manor house, down the road where the guerrillas were lying in wait.

"Beat it, Kristaps," Caleb muttered, shoving the kid behind the dais. But there was nowhere to hide.

The agent zeroed in on the boys and crossed the slushy cobblestones directly to where Eriks stood. A second Chekist came in on a bay, scouting the perimeter of the square at a brisk trot, followed by the third. The black horse fidgeted in front of Eriks, stamping close and blowing streams of white vapor. From the superior position of his saddle, the mounted agent assessed Eriks and Caleb. A brand spanking-new Russian submachine gun with a drum magazine hung from his shoulder. Eriks could see the wood grain on the oiled stock.

Caleb's hands rose in submission, but his stare conveyed all the frightening insolence that could be borne by a faceless, alien-eyed elk. His hand moved toward his head, perhaps to remove the mask and get some air.

"Took you long enough," Eriks told the agent, hoarsely.

The man on the black horse raised his rifle without a word, and with a *pa-pa-pa* and a bored expression, shot Caleb through the heart. Kristaps screamed.

A shot rang from across the square. Eriks dimly linked it with a jerk of the rider's belly and his slump over the saddle. The other horsemen pivoted and, banging hooves, charged the source of the bullet. From farther away gunfire peppered the air.

Staring at Caleb in horror, Eriks dropped to his knees. The black horse above him clattered against the cobblestones, nostrils flaring in panic. The dead weight of the Chekist careened out of the saddle and toppled, hanging a moment at the horse's flank before falling as the beast skittered across the square.

Eriks crawled to where Caleb lay, and wrenched the gasmask off his face. Uncut hair haloed Caleb's head on the ground. Complete surprise was frozen on his face, eyes wide at the sky, the starter moustache patchy over an o-shaped mouth. Eriks pressed an ear to Caleb's chest and heard a beat. But it was galloping horses pounding the ground. Caleb's heart was still. The snow was spreading crimson where he'd fallen, smelling like the butcher's shop.

The shooting on the road was furious. Eriks heard shouts. Aggrieved to leave Caleb, instinct bade his legs crawl to the dais and crouch, head under arms, listening. The longer he heard rifles firing, the more he knew his stupid plan had gone disastrously wrong, because his allies didn't have that many bullets. What had he thought? That those family men and their paltry arsenal would get the upper hand on the NKVD? The Cheka must've somehow taken cover and were right now rooting out and executing the brave fellows who'd been Silent Forest. His arrogance had killed Caleb. Next, the Cheka would find Eriks, the idiot mastermind, and kill him too. His parents would never know how his short thoughtless life had ended.

All fell quiet.

The stink of sulfur entered his throat.

The silence after the minutes of gunfire was unique, slowly broken by the sound of crisp, businesslike movement. They were coming for him. Too late to grab the rifle by the fallen horseman, Eriks was galvanized with fear. He saw the barrel of the gun first. At its other end stood Aivars.

Aivars eyed Eriks and Caleb, and nodded to someone else in the square, moving his hand in a series of gestures.

"Any Cheka in there?" Aivars demanded, pointing his weapon to the public house.

Eriks thought he answered, but maybe no sound came out, because Aivars kept asking.

"Just the local yoyos," Eriks finally said, as Aivars strode to the pub and kicked the door wide open. Snaggle-Wit and Stone Hill followed him inside, weapons drawn. He heard Aivars address the lunch crowd in a clear, angry tone.

"*Lab dien,* Villagers. Hear ye, hear ye. I got a message for any traitors here. To you party organizers and neighborhood spies and milk collectors. And I'm especially talking to you quiet go-along-to-get-along collaborators and lazy look-the-other-wayers. You are hereby directed to abandon your treacherous posts. The time has come for you to take a stand. I say return to your people. Join men in the forests unafraid of red scum or the cold. Swear to fight degenerate gangsters, so a Latvian can be the master of his own house."

As he listened to Aivars's ultimatum, Eriks watched Haralds, black frock coat billowing, kneel down and put two thin fingers to Caleb's neck. Then he swiftly passed his palm over Caleb's face, closing the eyes.

"Consider this your last warning," rang the voice of Aivars. "For whoever does not heed this directive, and does not return is Not Needed. And Shall Be sent straight to the Shade Mother."

The pub door slammed.

"Let's go, Eriks," Aivars called, already halfway across the square.

"Get up," Haralds said, pulling up Eriks by the arm.

Aivars picked up the dead horseman's assault rifle before leaving the square. Working as a pair, Snaggle and Stone stripped the uniform off the man who'd shot Caleb.

Haralds guided Eriks out of the village square, but when they reached the road, Eriks stopped and looked back. Caleb lay alone, but for the corpse of the mounted NKVD man who'd killed him, who in turn had been shot by the Hunter, laid out in the road just meters away, arms crossed over chest and head set to rest on a green-needled pine bough. The Hunter's killer was no doubt among the bodies strewn in the road.

"Keep going, Eriks," Haralds said, turning him firmly by the shoulders and forcing him forward. "There will be reprisals."

Eriks gazed down the road in a stupor, disconnected from its swift, methodical activity. Men were catching horses, plucking weapons and ammunition from lifeless figures in the snow, rolling bodies and peeling off their clothes. Kristaps was in the fray, tugging a boot from a leg of green wool.

Next thing Eriks knew he was standing near the Architect, who was holding the assault rifle as if weighing it against heavy considerations.

Captain Wagtail strode up leading three horses behind him. "Twenty," Wagtail told the Architect. "No fewer than twenty came out. Completely off guard. A masterstroke."

The Architect nodded. He held Eriks's eye like it was an induction ceremony, and pushed the PPS submachine gun to Eriks's chest, saying, "The *Papasha*."

The gun was repulsive to Eriks, still warm, and Caleb getting cold.

"That's *daddy*," said Snaggle-Wit in passing. "Don't point it at anyone 'til you're ready to shoot."

Eriks's eyes stung as the Architect and Wagtail walked away and he was left holding the coveted rifle. Homburg Haralds pushed him toward the trees.

"Well played, Eriks," said one of the Architect's sons, leading a booty-loaded horse past.

"He's a wanted man from here on out," Haralds said. "Better call him... Bear Slayer."

- 14 -

MARCH 21, 1941
THE SUMMERHOUSE

WEARING GABARDINE BREECHES OVER woolen long johns, Kārlis Pērkons cinched his belt to the tightest notch. He adjusted his glasses and watched himself in his bedroom mirror don the final accoutrement for Private, Red Army 24th Latvian Territorial Corps, a steel helmet. Before leaving, he slid his Art Academy matriculation card between the mirror and the frame. If ¾when he came home, he would find the card here and resume his studies in art. Then he closed the door to the bedroom he'd been sharing with Hugo Krumins.

His friends were in the kitchen, having caught the milk train immediately after school to be with him when he presented his head.

"Hugo's the sure bet for valedictorian," Vilz Zarins was saying, looking dark with slicked hair, seaman's cap and bomber jacket.

"Which means on top of exams I have to come up with a speech," Hugo said, white shirt, face and hair.

"Sucker!" Sniedze said, from under an oversized newsboy cap.

"If I'm not back for graduation, assume I've been killed," Kārlis said, going for merry banter but the comedy falling flat.

"With your boots on!" Jekabs Leopolds said, rescuing him. "Better than slain by Hugo's speech like the rest of us." That the Leopolds had come made Kārlis feel like a million *lats*, because he knew they always went to their temple on Friday evenings. Jekabs was rarely seen not working, but this afternoon he was in a sports coat instead of an apron and without a speck of flour from the top of his wavy haircut to the soles of his shiny shoes. His Uncle Eli was outside talking with Kārlis's father, the two avidly discussing ways to increase ventilation to the root cellar.

"Thanks for coming all this way," Kārlis said to all.

"We are the Nonchalants," Vilz said, in a fierce whisper, upholding her fist to the center of the group. "A Nonchalant will never abandon another Nonchalant."

"Or give up his name," Hugo said, copying the fist pose. "No matter how they torture you."

"Or steal his girl," Kārlis said.

"Sharply creased fedora, black-faced wristwatch, English newspaper," Jekabs said. "That was our style."

"While it lasted," Sniedze said. "Now we're the Nonchalants minus Peters and Eriks. And soon we'll be minus Kārlis."

Leave it to Sniedze to spoil the moment, Kārlis

thought, forgiving him. The twit couldn't help but blurt out any feeble thought that rose in his puny mind.

"Time to go," his mother called from the front hall. "We're in trouble if you miss the army train."

"I got it," Hugo said, offering to carry his duffel.

"Bring an umbrella, Biruta," called his mother. "It's a gray sky."

Kārlis heard his little sister's running steps as the Nonchalants filed out the kitchen door into a spring afternoon where all was wet and green with new growth bursting from every earthen crevice.

A rickety wooden ladder leaned against the linden tree, and on the top rung Kārlis recognized Tante Agata's rubber galoshes. She was muttering something, her arms and shoulders among the pliable branches and leaf buds dancing in the wind.

"Tante Agata, you're too high," Kārlis said, holding up a hand to steady her.

A flutter of blue silk brushed his arm as Tante Agata finished tying a ribbon around the tree. She grasped his hand, descending, and put her palm to the trunk. "Kārlis, you know your linden sister," she said, as if introducing him to a debutante at a ball. "You've grown up together. You can find her wherever they send you."

His eyes tingled. *Dammit.* He'd acted manly up to now. Kārlis didn't want to get gooey wondering if he'd see her old gray braid and woven headband again.

"No more sacred groves, of course," she said, patting the trunk, "burned and salted by pillaging knights, but she won't be driven from this land, and you must draw on her energy." Tante Agata slipped her foraging basket over her shoulders, and adjusted her chunky amber necklaces, murmuring,

"The flowers, bee's sweet julep, bloom in May,
Five to ten drops of tincture, in water thrice a day,
Brew flowers for infection,
The leaves soothe anxious tension
Wood ash for intestine
Lifts spirit from depression
The sap abounds in mucilage
from which sugar can be elaborated,
Bilious giddiness, loose bowels
and thrumming head alleviated,
In May the yellow flowers be in bloom... "

Kārlis knew the ending and recited it with her.

"Pick most the flowers for the tea
but leave some for the broom."

It suddenly dawned on Kārlis that Tante Agata's constant chanting had never been mindless. The cunning old bird had been trying to instruct him all along. He walked with her down the drive wondering if, one day, he'd even understand her baffling proverbs. Kārlis matched his gait to Tante Agata's mincing step, falling farther behind his parents and Mr. Leopolds, who led the procession, and the Nonchalants swaggering behind them four abreast. He took time to admire the crocus, hyacinth, and daffodil spotting the drive. Gravel crunched underfoot as Kārlis left home, heart beating like a military drum.

"I don't think there's enough linden tea on the planet to calm down the world's nervous tension, Auntie."

To that she uprooted a cushiony clump of bog moss and told him, "Field dressing! Oh, my," she said, eyeing a carpet of mushrooms. "Pink Bottoms. That's what we want for dinner. I'll catch you up, Kārlis." She left him with a face-wrinkling smile and, lifting her skirt, Tante Agata crossed tangles of overgrowth to enter the trees where shafts of light hit the forest floor at a steep angle, her galoshes sinking slightly into the thaw.

Kārlis's mother called from the front of the parade, "Biruta, don't step in those puddles!" The warning arrived just as his little sister jumped on his back, flinging arms around his neck and jarring his helmet. "Giddy-up!" she said, kicking her shoes.

He caught her legs, piggyback style, and trotted to catch up with the others who had by now turned onto the road leading to the village. Biruta disproved the maxim about the cobbler's children going shoeless. Janis Pērkons's daughter always had new shoes, even during the past year when no one did. Hers, slyly custom-crafted by the leather master at his father's confiscated Leather Works, were cream-colored saddle shoes with light blue piping. Kārlis would not be home to celebrate his sister's upcoming Name's Day, or to see her turn ten.

Just as he caught up with the boys, he observed Vilz Zarins tuck a paper into a mailbox. Kārlis turned on his heel, quick, hoping his little sister hadn't seen, and set her down. She laughed at the jerky stop that made her braids fly, and ran to catch up with their mother.

Kārlis snatched the leaflet, and turned his shoulder to read it unseen, instantly recognizing the raised "e" made by Vilz's typewriter.

"*Ak tu kungs!* Vilz! My sister almost saw you. You can't leaflet in this neighborhood. Someone might think it's my family spreading anti-Soviet dirt."

"One newspaper's worth a thousand firebombs," Vilz said, without apology.

"Yah. And just as dangerous if caught," Kārlis said, reading the handbill. "You wrote this?"

"Nay, a professor hiding in the Bikernieki wrote it," Vilz said. "But I came up with the title."

Latvia on Verge of Extinction

After nine months of Russian occupation, our confusion is past. By now everyone has seen relatives and friends arrested on the slimmest of suspicion and has grimly stayed silent.

We at first thought only "Harmful Elements" were to be reprimanded by the Communist regime. We now know we are dealing with cynical and cold-blooded minds that consider the whole independence-minded Latvian nation to be a Harmful Element.

As individuals we bear up, tottering under injustice. Collectively, Latvia is on the verge of being erased from the registry of nations.

Now that the destruction of Latvian values and order is well underway, the gloves are coming off. No longer bothering to wear the mask of legitimacy, how long before the Communists decide open slaughter is the simplest means to achieve their goal?

Will Germany arrive before the planned destruction of our nation is realized?

Kārlis gulped. Was Germany coming to save them? Bringing war, war with the Red Army? Kārlis looked at his Red Army uniform, stomach churning bilious giddiness, soft bowels and thrumming head. Nazis. That's who Kārlis would be sent to fight.

"Don't be afraid of Fritzes," Hugo said, reading over his shoulder. "The average Russian soldier fears what his own side will do to him more than Germans."

"That's comforting, Hugo," Kārlis said, resuming walking. "This is nuts. Things should never have gotten to this point. I should be graduating high school and going to the Art Academy. I should be screaming, running in the opposite direction as this army train, following Tante Agata into the woods, or hiding with the professor in the Bikernieki Forest. But that would leave my family having to answer to the Ivans."

They had reached the Bier Schtube, across from the train station, and stopped walking. Raindrops fell. A few customers seated on the outside tables were taking their beers and plates inside the tavern for shelter.

"The future's a loaded shotgun pointed at our heads," Vilz said.

"But they keep everybody going to work," Jekabs said. "Cook the frog gradually. If you just drop it in boiling water, it will leap out."

"Actually, the frog's skinny legs turn into a mess of thin, white strands," Sniedze said. "I know for a fact it just dies a nasty death."

"Get out of the rain, Kārlis," his mother called, from under the awning at the platform. "Janis, he's in the rain."

"Mama, I'm not made of sugar," Kārlis shouted, loitering in the road outside the Bier Schtube, watching the door. He wanted to see Lileja, wanted Lileja to see him in the soldier uniform.

"Her father won't let her out," Hugo said, reading his mind.

How did Hugo happen to know that, Kārlis wondered.

Janis Pērkons came over twirling his umbrella. He lifted Kārlis in a bear hug and set him down gasping, right in front of everybody. "If the world were ruled by women there'd be no war," he said, tilting his head at the Bier Schtube. "Just a couple nations not talking to each other. Did you know I married Mrs. Pērkons one week before I was called up to the Czar's Imperial Army," he said. "Then I spent four years in a German POW camp before seeing her again. She waited for me. I don't know if they make them like her anymore."

No, Kārlis guessed. That did not sound like Lileja.

Then a shutter swung open from the uppermost window, at the narrowest point of the steeply pitched roof. Waves of blonde hair tumbled forward as Lileja leaned out from the Bier Schtube. She smiled, waving down at Kārlis, and it felt like the sun had broken through.

"*Sveiks*, Lileja," Kārlis called, holding his helmet as he tipped his chin up and waved back, feeling a measure of peace flood his soul. He looked over his shoulder. Hugo was also waving, returning the smile. So was his father and every fellow in the road, smiling up at the window. Who had her smile been meant for? It didn't matter.

"Now would be a good time to go," his father said. And Kārlis followed him toward the platform.

"Mr. Pērkons." It was the stationmaster coming around the side of the building, dressed in a dark navy uniform with two columns of brass buttons and gold cording across the visor of his peaked cap.

"*Lab dien*, sir." Janis Pērkons greeted the stationmaster with a slap on the back. His father was on easy terms with the leaders of society.

"You're coming to the card game."

"Wouldn't miss it," Janis replied. "Say, what's this business here?" He pointed down the yard, to where cattle cars were stockpiled on the sidings.

The stationmaster lowered his voice. "They are retrofitting those for people."

His father's face fell, haggard within the symmetry of his sideburns and goatee.

"More of them each day," the stationmaster said. "Shuttling them between the smaller towns. An ill omen, I tell you."

Kārlis felt his guts wrench. The train was due in minutes and he had to use the toilet. He held back from following his father and the stationmaster as they ambled toward the vacated construction site, shaking heads at the wide shelving being installed in the cattle cars. Further down the track, black smoke billowed into the gloaming. The train was coming.

"I better say goodbye to Mama," Kārlis said, excusing himself.

The Nonchalants, Biruta and Mr. Leopolds were already filling up the small platform, huddled under umbrellas and looking, Kārlis feared, like an illegal assembly. Watching them was a burly, dark-haired man in a civilian overcoat, a rifle on his shoulder, local militia, extra police. His mother was wending her way toward the "self-defense" man, though Kārlis could not fathom why.

"You clean up well," Mrs. Pērkons told the burly militia-man, as Kārlis came over to stand by her. "I almost didn't recognize you."

The man recognized *her*. His deep-set eyes, shadowed by a protruding forehead, gleamed with interest.

"The lathe-and-plaster you repaired in my entryway," Mrs. Pērkons said. "It's flaking off. Could you possibly come take a look at it?"

"Is the old lady still at your place?" the militiaman asked in a gravelly voice. "The granny with the medicinals."

Kārlis froze, his guts roiling at the raspy voice. The coarse tone hurled him back to a harrowing episode from the winter. This man had stalked him, been on the opposite side of the noble oak, at the swing in the clearing, where Kārlis had hid with Lileja. He'd been ordered by a Russian to weed out keepers of the lore, like Tante Agata.

Mrs. Pērkons began, "She could remedy that hoarse—"

"No," Kārlis interrupted. "My great-Aunt doesn't live here anymore."

Massive locomotives pounded toward the station, filling ears with the roar of engines.

"She went back to Riga," Kārlis shouted to the militiaman, above the din. "I'll write you, Mama," Kārlis said, flinging his arms around his mother's shoulders. He maneuvered her away, whispering, "Steer clear of that one. He's trouble."

The engines slowed, dragging passenger carriages past the platform, dominating space with noise and iron.

"He's my handyman," she whispered. "He's always been a pariah." His mother spoke fast, while brakes screeched. "No one would hire him when he got out of prison a couple years ago for manslaughter, except your father."

Kārlis nodded. His father was on easy terms with the dregs of society. But his father didn't know what Kārlis knew.

"Janis gave him odd jobs until he got on his feet," his mother said.

The train crawled forward amid pneumatic hisses, finally stopping. The door to Kārlis's carriage swung open. This was a whistlestop and Kārlis the only passenger.

"Well, he's militia now, so stay away from him," he told her, tersely. "Keep him away from Auntie."

Kārlis looked up, startled to see the militia-man standing right beside him. He kissed his mother's forehead and announced, "I already fixed that plaster, Mama. I should've shown you but I forgot in my rush to join the army." He met the man's deep-set eyes. "So it's not a problem."

The man lowered his head, studying Kārlis. Something further was expected.

"The eagle doesn't catch flies," Kārlis told him, quoting Tante Agata, and shrugging his eyebrows.

It was time to board.

Ak tu kungs! Convicts running the town. Grannies wanted for arrest. Artists turned to soldiers. Cattle cars for people. The world was a spinning shambles.

Hugo gave him the duffle. Someone dressed like Kārlis but with black *gorgets*, stepped onto the platform, shoulders squared, and matched Kārlis's document to information on a roster. Kārlis was admitted on board, bound for the Litene training camp nine hours hence, pure, grade-A Latvian cannon fodder.

Arms stretched out to Kārlis as he mounted the train, fingers and palms imparting the content of hearts.

Sveiks, Kārlis. *Sveiki.*

The stationmaster blew his whistle. The train left the station.

Kārlis barely had time to slough his duffle in an empty seat and crane his neck to the window where his life, standing along the platform, shot by in a blur. The Bier Schtube, the road to the village, Tante Agata's woods, the summerhouse, the linden tree, all dissolved into a budded forest about to riot.

But the light lingered. Shafts bore through the nimbus hinting at mysteries hidden in the trees. Today was the vernal equinox, with exactly equal lengths of light and dark. The sun would set precisely at 18:28. There was still that much order in the universe.

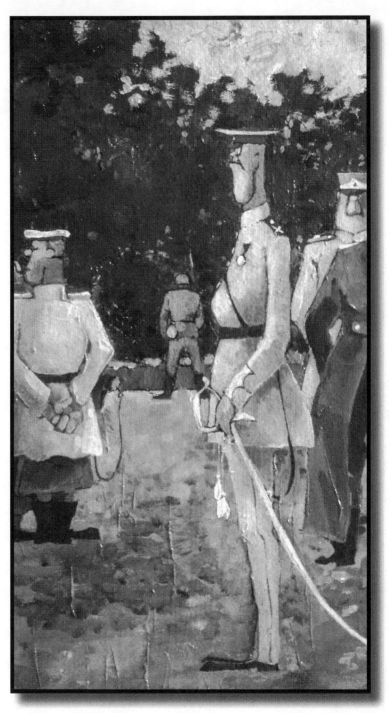

K. Smiltens, 1950.

Epilogue

"AND THAT, MUZAIS PUISITS, IS *how I learned to make this tea,*" *Kārlis Pērkons said. He collected the empty teacup, and turned off the bedside lamp.* "Feeling better?"

The flushed face bobbed as Kārlis moved toward the door.

"Wait, Uncle Kārlis," *came the high voice from the pillow.* "Is Latvia a real place?"

Kārlis stopped midstride. "Of course it's real," *he said.* "Why would you even ask me that?"

"The Mysterious Island's not a real place." *His nephew sat up, putting a small hand on the Jules Verne tome Kārlis often read.* "No one at school has heard about Latvia, not even my teacher."

Kārlis struggled to find the right words. Events from his former life were still vivid enough to wake him in a midnight sweat. "It's real all right."

"So is Tante Agata still alive?" the little boy asked. "Did Lileja marry Hugo after you left? Did Peters ever come back?"

"I don't know," Kārlis said, "but I search every issue of the Exile Examiner for news."

"Can't you write and find out?"

"If they received a letter from someone in America," Kārlis said, "they would be arrested for spying."

"Just for getting a letter?" The boy stared, wide-eyed. "That's not proof. Then anybody could be arrested."

Kārlis leaned against the doorjamb with a sigh. Compared to his hulking frame, everything in the room seemed small. Stilts. Rockets. Dinosaurs. How could a little boy possibly understand? "Sounds crazy," he said with a half-hearted shrug. "But I promise you, it's real."

"Then where did Grandfather bury the treasure?"

Kārlis fumbled, barely catching the clattering cup and saucer.

"Grandfather Janis," the boy insisted. "That part's real too then. Right? Where did he bury it?"

Kārlis's eye darted to the window and scanned the hallway outside the boy's room. No one was there. He exhaled. "I've already said too much."

The television set was droning from the living room. Kārlis had turned it on, anxious to watch the 5:30 newscast. Cuba had been invaded by a mercenary force, which Fidel Castro claimed was organized, financed and armed by the US government. Lurking behind Castro was the tall shadow of the Soviet Union, the only nation besides America with the atomic bomb. Communism, it seemed, had chased Kārlis across the globe to the Bay of Pigs, practically on American shores. But this time the thugs would not catch him unawares.

"Don't talk about this to anybody, muzais puisits." Kārlis said, recognizing a lifelong wave of dread as he raised his finger to his lips. "Never speak of these things."

Parade of the Dead. K. Smiltens, 1948.

When not writing, the author loves ethnic folk dance.

Sveiks!

Thank you for looking at my book.

My friends shook their heads, muttering *insane* and *swallowing a watermelon* when I publicly committed to a twelve book historical fiction series. But that's the breadth and depth of the story, so wish me luck.

I married into Latvia, rushing to the library soon after meeting my future mother-in-law because I knew nothing of her homeland. In 1992, we were among the earliest expats returning to the country, newly independent after fifty years of tyranny. Our tour guides were Uncle Kārlis's high school friends, two who had survived. They brought me face to face with a living history that, growing up in sunny southern California, I never imagined. That first visit forever changed my understanding of freedom, democracy and the human spirit.

Kārlis Smiltens, de facto War Artist of the Latvian Legion, died in 2017. His paintings allow us a glimpse into the thoughts of a young man coming of age during the crisis of 1940 Latvia. You can see the full and color versions at www.DianaMathur.com. Drop me a line at the website. I'd love to hear from you.

With Vigilance,

Diana Mathur

Bibliography

The following resources are acknowledged: *The Unknown War, The Latvian National Partisans Fight Against the Soviet Occupiers, 1944-1956* by Gunārs Blūzms et al, HPT Ltd., 2011, *Latvian Religion, An Outline*, Jānis Dārdedzis, Baltic Crossroads, Los Angeles, 1996, Museum of the Occupation of Latvia, *Latvia in World War II Catalogue-Guidebook of the Latvian Military Museum* by Valdis Kuzmins, *The Forgotten War, Latvian Resistance During the Russian and German Occupations* by Janis Straume, *Baltic Amber* by Inara Mantenieks, *Latvian Legion* by Arthur Silgailis, *Memoires of a Partisan* by Y. Sigaltchik, *In the Partisan Detachment* by Shmuel Margolin, *Laima Veckalne's Story: A Tale of Forgotten Soviet Crimes* by Edgar B. Anderson, *M16: Inside the Covert World of Her Majesty's Secret Intelligence Service* by Stephen Dorril, *Latvia: Year of Horror* by Baigais Gads, *Latvia in the Wars of the 20th Century* by Visvaldis Mangulis, *Hitler versus Stalin* by Professor John & Ljubica Erickson, *Landscape as an Indicator of Art Life in Latvia During the Period of Nazi Occupation* by Janis Kalnacs, www.cyberussr.com by Hugo S. Cunningham, *Occupation of Latvia by Nazi Germany, Forest Brothers* and *Baltic Way* by Wikipedia, *2X2 Divisions* by Frank Gordon from www.centropa.org, *Latvian Legion at Lake ILMENA* from www.lacplesis.com, Welcome to Latvia-Folk Songs from the Latvian Institute, www.li.lv, *These Names Accuse—Nominal List of Latvians Deported to Soviet Russia* by The Latvian Foundation, and *The Baltic Observer* since 1996 known as *The Baltic Times*.

Diligent effort has been made to acknowledge sources correctly. Any errors or unintentional omissions will be corrected in future editions of this book.

Paldies!

Thank you, Biruta Smiltens Mathur,
for stories about growing up in Latvia.

This book is a credit to Kris Mathur and his
unflagging support.

Barbara Peterson, Editor
Georgia Saroj, Illustrator

Signe Irbe and Aivars Riekstins, tour guides at the
Corner House, Museum of the Occupation of Latvia
in Riga, have impacted this story directly.

Gretchen Holzhauer-Irwin, Madeline Irwin and Penelope Irwin,
thanks for your friendship, time and opinions.

Paldies to Astra Moore for her careful
historical and cultural critique of past manuscripts.

Arijs and the late Anta Krievins,
contributed riveting details.
Thank you, Rita Sharpe and family.

A toast to the irregulars at Café Mimosa,
to Joey Ector and his flute.

Propers to James Mathers, Rodeo Grounds Poet Laureate.

Glossary

Ak tu kungs! (AWK-te KOONKS) Oh my Lord! Give me patience!

Apakšbikses (UP-iksh-BIK-shes) Underpants

Baltics Countries surrounding the Baltic Sea: Lithuania, Latvia, Estonia (also Finland)

Besom A tied-twig sauna bath switch for whipping, stimulating and exfoliating the skin

Bier Schtube A bier stube is a hall or pub that specializes in beer, German. In the story, Bier Schtube is a proper noun and purposely misspelled to clue readers to its pronounciation.

Bolshevik Russian political party that embraced Lenin's Communist thesis

Budēļi A masked, house-to-house, animal-honoring, musical folkloric procession enjoyed from St. Martin's Day through Shrove Tuesday

Cheka Another name for the NKVD

Corner House NKVD headquarters in Riga. In 1940, 700 "Undesirables" at a time were secretively incarcerated in this fashionable art nouveau building.

Cilvēk (SIL-vak) Human being, dude, Latvian

Dacha (DAH-kuh) Country house or villa, Russian

Daina (DAY-en-uh) Traditional form of uniquely Latvian music or poetry

Daugava (DOW-guh-vuh) Latvia's longest river, running through Riga to the Baltic Sea

Deita (DEE-eh-tuh) the house cow, Latvian for daisy.

Kakis (KAT-kis), Latvian for cat and the name of Biruta's cat

Kapost galva (KAP-ust GAUL-vuh) Stands for vulgar, teenaged slang. Use your imagination.

Kulak (KOO-lak) A peasant wealthy enough to own a farm and hire labor. Millions were arrested, exiled, or killed under Stalin's forced collectivization, Russian

Lats (LOTS) Latvian currency

Lāčplēsis (LOCKS-pleesh) Mythical giant Bear-Slayer acclaimed in the epic poem by Andrejs Pumpurs, who based the nationalistic hero on existing Latvian folklore.

Witch Hammer

Loudzu (LEWDZ-u) Please, and You're Welcome

Malleus Maleficarum (The Hammer of the Witches) A blood-soaked 1486 guidebook to aid Inquisitors in the identification, prosecution, and dispatching of Witches, especially poets, midwives, and widow landowners, Latin

Midsummer Summer solstice, revered and raucous Latvian holiday

Muzais puisits (MUZ-ice PWEE-seets) Little boy

NKVD Abbreviation for Narodnyi Komissariat Vnutrennikh Del, Народный комиссариат внутренних дел, The People's Commissariat for Internal Affairs, i.e. the Communist secret police, later known as the KGB

Name's Day The day of the year to celebrate a particular name and its bearers

The Nonchalants Seven friends in mortal danger for coming of age under Stalin's occupation

Paldies (paul-DEE-es) Thank you

Pie joda (PEE-eh YO-duh) To the devil

Pirts A traditional wood-fired sauna with steam

Проклятье (Proklyat'ye) Curse, an imprecation that great harm or evil may befall someone, Russian

Red Army Army of the Soviet Union, Russia, the Communists

Riga (REE-guh) Capital of Latvia

The **Servant Attacks with saw and Axe The Lumber, Stack and Cord** A mnemonic device for the vertebral column: Cervical (Atlas, Axis) Thoracic, Lumbar, Sacral, Caudal. Inventor unknown.

Стой, или вы будете расстреляны! (Stoy, ili vy budete rasstrelyany!) Stop, or you will be shot!, Russian

Sveiks (SVAYkes) Hello and See you later

The Pērkonses: It's only a matter of time, but being optimists, they always hope for one more day.

THE PERKONSES

AGATA

JANIS   ANNA

KARLIS   BIRUTA

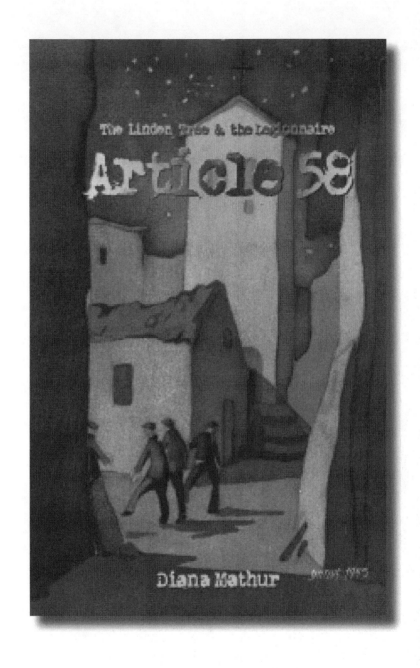

The Linden Tree & the Legionaire

Article 58

Diana Mathur

Book I: *Article 58*
Available through Barnes & Noble.com, Amazon,
and wherever books are sold

The Linden Tree & the Legionnaire

Witch Hammer

Diana Mathur

Book II: *Witch Hammer*
*Available through Barnes & Noble.com, Amazon,
and wherever books are sold*

Book III: *The Knock at Night*
Available through Barnes & Noble.com, Amazon,
and wherever books are sold

The Ghastly Year

Diana Mathur

Books I - III: *The Ghastly Year*
Available through Barnes & Noble.com, Amazon,
and wherever books are sold

Coming Soon!

Made in the USA
Las Vegas, NV
30 September 2023

78359483R00116